THEY CALLED HIM RABBONI

By
Helen Thornton

Illustrated by
Janice Ross

PublishAmerica
Baltimore

© 2008 by Helen Thornton.
All rights reserved. No part of this book may be reproduced, stored in a retrieval system or transmitted in any form or by any means without the prior written permission of the publishers, except by a reviewer who may quote brief passages in a review to be printed in a newspaper, magazine or journal.

First printing

This is a work of fiction. Names, characters, places, and incidents either are the product of the author's imagination or are used fictitiously. Any resemblance to actual persons, living or dead, events, or locales is entirely coincidental.

PublishAmerica has allowed this work to remain exactly as the author intended, verbatim, without editorial input.

ISBN: 1-60441-342-5
PUBLISHED BY PUBLISHAMERICA, LLLP
www.publishamerica.com
Baltimore

Printed in the United States of America

DEDICATION

To the Glory of HaShem

ACKNOWLEDGMENTS

Firstly, Ruach Ha'Kodesh, the Holy Spirit, Who is the real author of this book. I am just the scribe.

My parents, Tim and Doro Thorpe, who brought me up 'in the nurture and admonition of the Lord', and who kept a thesaurus within reach at the dining room table. Dad taught me to appreciate the nuances of the English language.

Janice, my illustrator, and our husbands, Ian and Errol; our cheering section, for their love and encouragement, and their belief in this project.

I have been fortunate to have been able to listen to some great teachers, among them Dr. Daniel Juster and Joe Amaral, whose words triggered a need to understand the background of Jesus' life. In particular I owe a debt to Dr. Alistair Petrie, who has taught me many things over many years,

I am grateful to Jill Veitch and Moreh Dalla Porta for their expertise. Dr. Ketriel Blad's Messianic Torah Commentary was an invaluable resource.

Thank you, I love and appreciate you all.

TABLE OF CONTENTS

Introduction   *9*

Prologue   *11*

Do You Remember?   13

Interlude   18

Background—A Jewish Boyhood   *25*

My Sheep…   27

Pressed Down and Running Over   32

In My Father's House   38

Grafted In   43

Ari's Special Day   49

Chanukah   55

Pesach   62

Gone Fishin'   68

Rabboni   *75*

Ari's Snack   77

Two by Two	84
The Woman from Samaria	92
Storyteller	99
Odd Man Out	105
Hosannah	111
The Hidden Disciple	117
153 Fish	124
Epilogue	***129***
Shavuot	131
Go into All the World	139
Glossary of Names	***145***

INTRODUCTION

In this book I have attempted to portray the Galilee as it was in the time of Jesus. I have tried to strip away two thousand years of history and show what it was really like to live and work there and experience the culture of the times.

The Ari stories were the first ones written in an effort to show this culture, and they form a background to the Rabboni stories which follow.

In the first century of this era there were no names like Peter, James and John, so I am using, so far as is possible, the original names for the Biblical characters. Many of them are not familiar to modern readers, so a glossary of these names is included at the back. Most of the names are either Hebrew or Aramaic, but some exceptions, such as Philippos and Stephanos, are Greek, since there are no Hebrew or Aramaic equivalents, and there was a considerable Greek influence in the Middle East in the first century A.D.

I have also included a short passage of explanation or enlargement at the end of each story. Sometimes it puts these incidents into the larger picture.

I have tried to write only what the Holy Spirit told me to write, so the mistakes that I have made are mine alone.

PROLOGUE

SHEPHERD

DO YOU REMEMBER?

The three elderly men sat huddled around a small fire in the courtyard. They pulled their cloaks around them against the chill of the evening. Their gnarled hands gripped their shepherd's crooks—they would have felt lost without them to hold, but these days they used the crooks more to keep their balance than to herd sheep. They had spent many years out on the hillsides near Beit Lechem, but their flocks had long since passed into younger hands, and nowadays they had little to do but keep themselves warm.

Thaddeus, Eli and Dan'yyel sat around swapping stories, as old men do, and if some of the tales were embellished beyond fact, well, that just made them more interesting. But there was one story which would never need embroidering; the truth was still so remarkable, even after so many years had passed.

It was a beautiful evening, clear and cool, in the fall of the year. The stars shone like brilliants in a canopy of velvet, and in the east there was a lightening in the sky as the moon was rising.

"Do you remember?" mused Eli, as he gazed at the starry sky. "That night when the angel came?" His companions nodded eagerly; they all remembered that night so clearly. "It was Moshe who first saw him." There had been four of them at that time, but Moshe was the first to leave them, having succumbed to a bad cough the previous winter.

"Look!" Moshe had said. "There is a man standing there. He's huge, and he seems to glow. Maybe he is an angel!" They all looked at what Moshe had seen. There was a bright light surrounding the man, who was dressed in white. The shepherds recoiled, falling on their faces and trembling in fear. The angel spoke to them;

"Don't be afraid," he said. "I am here to tell you something that will bring great joy to you and many others. Tonight in the City of Dawid, a child has been born. He will be a Savior to you, and He is the Mashiach. Look for him in a stable, where you will find Him wrapped in swaddling clothes and lying in a manger."

The four men sat up and looked at the angel and at each other, wonder and confusion shining in their eyes. This did not make a whole lot of sense; a Savior born in a stable? Their thoughts were interrupted when a whole crowd of angels appeared, singing with one voice,

"Glory to El Shaddai, and peace to men on earth."

The angels disappeared, and the shepherds looked around them. There was nothing there but the dark night, and the sheep grazing quietly as though nothing had happened. They could not get over their experience, and began to discuss what they had seen and heard.

"I just don't understand this," murmured Thaddeus, "this must be the long-awaited Mashiach they are talking about, but surely a king would be born in a palace, not in a stable. Maybe we had better go and check this out. The sheep will be all right for a while; I'll tell young Dawid to keep an eye on them; he slept through all the excitement." They gathered up their shepherds' crooks, wrapped their cloaks tightly around them, picked up a couple of orphan lambs they needed to watch, and set off for Beit Lechem in some excitement.

"But how are we going to find this place?" complained Eli. "Beit Lechem is full of people this week, here for both the census and Sukkot."

Then something new appeared in the sky, which had not been visible earlier; a bright star which they had thought was the moon about to rise. It seemed to move, and then to hover in one particular place.

"That could be a sign," suggested Dan'yyel. "Let's follow it and see what happens."

The three shepherds hurried towards Beit Lechem, the City of Dawid, where it had long been prophesied that the Mashiach would be born. The streets were crowded with people, but they pushed their way through, trying to keep the star in sight. The star seemed to grow closer and brighter as they ran, until finally they came to a mean street, where there were several inns, all full of pilgrims. There seemed to be a glow coming from one particular opening, and when they reached it and looked inside, they could see a young couple gazing tenderly at a manger full of straw, where a newborn baby lay sleeping, wrapped in cloths.

The men approached cautiously, realizing that what they had been told by the angels was true, and that this baby was indeed the Savior of the world, come in human form. They knelt and worshipped Him, and then spoke with His parents. Miriam and Yosef had come from Natzarat in the Galilee, but could not find room in an inn, so had to wander the streets, with Miriam on a donkey, knowing that her time had come, until an innkeeper had taken pity on them and given them some room and privacy in a stable. His wife had been able to assist Miriam, and when the baby was born they laid Him in the manger for lack of a more appropriate cradle, and called Him Yeshua, as they had been told to do. The innkeeper's ox and Yosef's donkey kept guard, and only they knew what they thought of all this.

When the shepherds left, they were full of excitement about this turn of events, and could not help telling people they met about what had taken place. They remembered from their study of the scriptures that this had in fact been foretold, many hundreds of years before, so they praised Yahweh and glorified Him. Miriam however, though she knew Yeshua was the Son of HaShem, pondered this all over again, in bewilderment that she was the one who had been chosen to be the mother of the Savior.

Thaddeus, Eli and Dan'yyel returned to the present, to the cool evening in their old age.

"It was just such a night as this," commented Dan'yyel, "at this time of the year. It must be thirty years ago now, or maybe a bit more. I remember that it was while that evil man Herod was king. He got jealous when he heard that another King had been born, and ordered all the young children to be killed. They took my precious son, my Shimon, my youngest."

"And mine," murmured Eli sadly. "Those were dark days. I wonder did Yeshua and his family escape, and what became of them. If He is still alive he must be a man now."

"You know," mused Thaddeus, "my son was telling me the other day that there is a new teacher who is going around, talking about the Kingdom of Heaven, and how He is The Way to that kingdom. He would be about the right age, and His name is Yeshua, I have been told. My son's friend Stefanos from Yerushalayim keeps disappearing for days at a time, and then comes back talking in glowing terms about this man and His teaching. It could be the same person we saw as a little baby so long ago. Has the Mashiach really arrived, so you suppose?"

They discussed this for a while, and then Marta, Thaddeus' wife, approached the trio bearing a basket of fruit which she set down within their reach.

"Are you three going to talk all night?" she asked. "I for one am going to bed. It's getting late." They talked for a few more minutes as they helped themselves to figs and dates, then Dan'yyel and Eli struggled to their feet with the aid of their crooks.

"We must go."

"We are keeping you up."

"Goodnight. See you tomorrow." They shuffled off down the street, two elderly shepherds, one tall and one short, arm in arm for balance, towards their own houses not far away, still talking about what had happened on the most exciting evening of their lives.

There is no evidence that it was a star which showed the way to the place where Jesus was born, but I have included it as a way for the shepherds to locate the stable. Jerusalem was full of people and no one would have been able to direct the shepherds because no one else knew about His birth. Therefore a supernatural guide was needed so that they could find Him.

INTERLUDE

Miriam cuddled her tiny baby, holding Him close to her breast. She was just enjoying Him, and marveling at Who He was. Yeshua was just a few weeks old, and several days ago she and Yosef had taken Him to the temple where they had met Shimon and Anna, both of whom had recognized Him as the future Mashiach. While in the temple they completed their ritual purification, and offered a sacrifice of two pigeons, because they could not afford a lamb.

She smiled across the room at her cousin Elisheva, who was bouncing her own six month old son, Yochanon, on her lap. The two mothers, one very young, the other much older, were content in the company of their children. Yosef leant against the wall, smiling indulgently at the peaceful scene. He had finished his work for the day, and his wages were in his pouch. They had recently moved into lodgings in Beit Lechem, Elisheva was visiting them for a few days while her husband Zecharya fulfilled his priestly duties at the temple, and all was right with Yosef's world.

Later that evening they had some strange visitors. There was a knock on the outer door. They looked up, startled. Who was coming to them at this hour? Yosef opened the door a crack and was astounded to see a bright light shining on three exotic looking men, dressed in rich clothes, holding something in their hands. In the street he could see a number of other men with a string of camels.

"Yes?" he asked.

One of the men said. "Is this where the King of the Jews is living? We have seen His star in the east, and have come to worship Him." Yosef was somewhat taken aback, but opened the door wide and the three foreigners entered. Seeing Miriam and the Child, they fell to their knees, worshipped Him and humbly presented their gifts; gold, frankincense and myrrh. Elisheva and Yochanon watched from the shadows.

After their business was concluded, the three men talked with Yosef. They told him that they were astronomers from an eastern country, who had seen this new star and understood that it represented the newborn King of the Jews. They had spent several months in journeying to where the star was leading them, and when they reached Yerushalayim they went first to the palace of King Herod, expecting to find the new king there. Herod professed to know nothing of the matter, but asked them to let him know when they found the one they were seeking, so that he too could worship at His feet.

This made Yosef very uneasy; Herod did not have a good reputation, and was unlikely to take this news lightly. After the men left he discussed the matter with his wife and her cousin before they all retired for the night.

During the night Yosef had a dream. It seemed that an angel of HaShem was with him in his room, speaking to him;

"Do not stay here in Beit Lechem. Herod wants to find Yeshua to kill Him, so take the young Child and His mother, with all your possessions, and go down into Mitzrayim. Go now, at once, before the news gets around. HaShem will be with you and will guide you along the way."

Yosef awoke, realizing that he had been warned and would have to obey. He roused the women and told them what had happened. Miriam was scared, but Elisheva calmed her, saying,

"Do what you have to do. I will stay until the morning, and explain to the landlord that you had to leave in a hurry, and then I will take Yochanon and go to the cave in Ein Karem where we will stay until the danger is over. The soldiers will never find us there." Yosef and Miriam packed up their few possessions, including Yosef's carpentry tools and what food they had, and wrapping the magis' gifts in their clothing, they loaded everything onto their donkey. Miriam rode on the donkey, with Yeshua snug in her arms, while Yosef set out on foot.

They left Beit Lechem before dawn, traveling south, full of trepidation and wondering how they would be able to manage. They would have to travel on byroads if the soldiers were looking for them, and would have to rely on HaShem for protection and guidance.

As they walked south they realized that they would need to stay on the main road for a while, until they had left the vicinity of Beit Lechem. In the distance, as day was dawning, they could see ahead of them a Roman checkpoint. There was no way around it, so they would have to pass it, but recognized that Herod would not yet know he had been duped by the magi returning home another way, so there would be little danger as yet.

With Miriam holding the Baby tight so He would not announce their presence by crying, they approached the checkpoint quietly. The guard appeared to be asleep so they planned to pass by without speaking, and if necessary to bluff their way through. He was wakened though by the clop, clop of the donkey's hooves as they went through, but when he looked, he could see nothing.

"Hey," he called out. "Anybody there?" There was no answer, so he asked his companion if he had heard anything. They agreed that they had heard the animal's footsteps, but there was nothing at all to be seen. They shook their heads, thinking they must have imagined it, and then forgot all about it as they went about their daily business of checking passersby.

When they felt they were safe, on a lesser road, Yosef stopped the donkey in a shady place, so they could rest awhile and eat.

Miriam told her husband, "You know, I believe that I have an uncle in Mitzrayim, in Marmorica. Yosef is the younger brother of my father Yoachim, and he is a merchant who lives in that area. Perhaps we should try and find him and ask him for shelter." Yosef agreed that this would be a good idea, and that they would do as Miriam suggested.

They stayed in the shade of the oasis for the rest of the day, their only companions, briefly, a Bedouin family traveling in the opposite direction. Then as the heat of the day started to decrease, and Miriam rummaged in the saddle bags to see what food she could find, she turned and gasped as she spied a meal laid out for them on a flat rock; fruit and bread.

"Look!" she cried to Yosef, "HaShem has provided for us!" They gave thanks to HaShem and ate gratefully, before starting out again on their journey. They continued on their way south, traveling in the early morning and the cool of the evening, and resting during the heat of the day, with HaShem providing food for them morning and evening.

Once they crossed the Wadi of Mitzrayim, they were out of Herod's territory, and felt free to show themselves more openly. They stopped at the first village they entered and enquired for the town of Marmorica. Nobody there knew anything, so they continued to travel south until they could get directions to its whereabouts. Then, as they finally approached this community they started asking people if they knew of Yosef ben Matthias, who they said was a merchant. After asking around for a while they found someone who could tell them where this man lived, and they thankfully made their way there.

A knock at the door of the house to which they had been directed brought a servant who agreed that Yosef ben Matthias did indeed live there, and was at home. They were shown into a comfortable room with rich furnishings and the servant went to tell his master that Yosef ben Yaaq'ov and his family had arrived. The older Yosef was overjoyed to discover that these were truly kinsmen, Miriam being the daughter of his older brother Yoachim. The small family was made welcome, and shown to guest quarters where they were able to clean up and rest after their arduous journey.

At the evening meal the whole story was shared, and Yosef ben Matthias told them that he had heard through his contacts that King Herod was very angry that the magi had not reported to him before leaving, and that he had given orders that all male children in Beit Lechem under the age of two years were to be slaughtered, in order to make sure that there would be no new King of the Jews. This saddened them, and made them concerned for Elisheva and Yochanon, though they did not live in Beit Lechem, but had planned to hide out in the cave in Ein Karem. They gave thanks to HaShem that their small family had managed to escape.

Yosef and Miriam and Yeshua settled down contentedly in Marmorica under the protection of her uncle. Yosef found work as a carpenter and time passed happily. Then several months later word came that Herod had died, and at the same time Yosef was told in another dream that it would be safe to return to their own land, as those who had been seeking to kill the young Child were doing so no longer.

The young family took leave of their relative and made their way north up the coastal route which was shorter. Yosef of Marmorica sent several of his servants with them to ease their way, along with camels to carry them and their belongings. They decided that Beit Lechem was not where they wanted to live, since Archilaus was reigning in his father's place, and his reputation was no better than Herod's. So they continued north into Galilee to the town of Natzarat, Yosef's home town, where they settled down. Yosef re-opened his carpenter's shop and Miriam made a home for him and young Yeshua, who continued to grow strong. They had other children and became a normal family, except that Yosef and Miriam knew that Yeshua, their oldest, had a destiny that was beyond anything they could understand.

Legend tells us that Joseph of Arimathea was also known as Joseph of Marmore since he lived in Mitzrayim for a while as a young man. He was not very much older than his niece Mary, and became a wealthy merchant and provider of metals to the Roman Government. Other legends say that while he was indeed Mary's uncle it was through her mother; that he was brother to both Anna and to Bianca, who became mother to Elizabeth. The truth of the matter is open to discussion, depending on which ancient documents one reads or believes. One day, when we reach heaven, it will all be sorted out, and complicated relationships made clear. Marmorica no longer exists, and its whereabouts are unknown.

BACKGROUND—
A Jewish Boyhood

MY SHEEP...

Ari really missed his Dad!
Shemu'el was a shepherd—he tended his flock of sheep and watched over them. Unfortunately there was little pasture near the village where he lived with his family, so he had to take them to a valley about a day's walk away, where the grass was green and water was plentiful. He was often away for weeks at a time.
Ari stayed behind with his mother, Myriam, his older sister Sarah and the younger children. He was a great help to her in the afternoons. In the mornings he and the other village boys went to the house of the rabbi, to study the Torah and other writings. In a few months he would be old enough to become bar-mitzvah, and he really needed to study in order to prove to people that now he was ready to become a man. But he also enjoyed just being a boy among his friends, playing games in the village around the stone houses, and developing the skills he would need when he grew up.
But Ari missed Shemu'el badly and longed to talk to him—man talk. He was tired of listening to Myriam and the other women as they gossiped round the well in the middle of the village. He needed his Abba!

One day he approached his mother. "Ima, do you think I could go and see Abba for a few days? I am old enough now to walk there by myself. I promise to see that there is enough wood chopped for the cooking fire, and do any other chores that you need before I go. I will not stay long, but I do need to talk to my father."

Myriam was silent for a few moments and then said thoughtfully, "I suppose you are old enough now—you need to be with the other men for a while."

Ari was overjoyed, and hurried to do everything that was necessary to leave them supplied while he was away.

Early next morning he tied the straps on his sandals, bundled up his warm cloak—he would need it when he slept on the hard ground that night—took the food and water Myriam had prepared for his lunch, and put that and a few supplies for his father into a bag which he carried on his shoulder. He took up his staff, said a fond farewell to his family and bravely set out.

Myriam called after him, "Are you sure you know the way?"

"Yes," he replied, and pointed to a hill some distance away. "I keep walking towards the grove of trees on the top of that hill, and when I get there I should be able to see the sheep in the valley below."

"Go with Hashem" she answered, and turned away, her eyes misting. Her son was growing up and would not need her much longer.

Ari walked away with mixed feelings; he hated to leave his mother with the young ones, but he needed to go, too. It was hot and dusty, and grew hotter as the day advanced. As he walked he looked around at the rocks and scrubby bushes, and wondered if he would be lucky enough to see a hyrax, or rock rabbit, sunning himself on a high rock. He rummaged in his bag for his sling, picked up a few smooth pebbles from the path, and practiced throwing them at various targets along the way. He was getting quite skilled, and dreamed about the day when he would be able to drive away wild animals from those he loved. He tried to remember all that he saw, so that he could report to his father when he saw him.

Ari met a few people on the path, greeting them politely and stepping to one side so they could get past him, but for the most part he was quite alone with the birds and small animals. He whistled as he walked along to keep his spirits up, and from time to time he comforted himself by reciting passages from the Torah; he needed to have it all memorized and understood in time for his bar-mitzvah.

At noon, when the sun was high, he reached a small village where his aunt Rachel lived, and where he drank from his goatskin bag, and sat in the shade of a locust tree to eat his lunch and rest while he chatted with his relatives.

When he stood up to continue his journey he was much refreshed, and knew he could reach his father's camp by evening. He was glad to arrive at the top of the hill after quite a climb, and shifted his bag to the other shoulder. This thing was heavy! He looked back at the way he had come, and realized how far he had traveled since he set out that morning. He went through the trees and was happy to see the large flock of sheep grazing on the slopes below him. He started to run, and then spotted his father with the sheep, carrying his shepherd's crook and watching his flock.

"Abba!" he called when he was near enough, and Shemu'el heard him, and ran to catch his son in his arms.

"Ari," he cried, "Is everything all right at home?" Are Myriam and the children well?"

"Oh yes," Ari answered, "Everything is fine, and all are keeping well. But I had to see you, and my ima said I was old enough to come by myself for a few days." Shemu'el gave him a big hug, which Ari returned with a grin.

Father and son had a joyful reunion, talking as they walked with the sheep, and Ari commented on the large number in the flock.

"Are they all ours?" he asked.

"No." replied his father. "There are four of us shepherds here with our sheep. Come and meet the others." They found Dan'yyel, Yonatan and Shimon sitting around their campfire, cooking supper for them all.

The evening was spent in great company, Ari being treated like an equal among men for the first time in his life. The four men told stories around the campfire, stories about their experiences among the sheep. One told of the time they watched an irate and determined sheep face down and then chase off a marauding fox which had planned to make a meal of her lamb.

Then as it started to grow dark Shemu'el said to his son,

"It is time to move the sheep to their fold for the night. There are many wolves and other wild animals who would love to attack the sheep while no-one is watching them. See that enclosure on the hill behind us?" Ari looked and saw a rough enclosure built from rocks and thornbushes, with a single opening at one end. "Come and help me."

"But how do you know which sheep are yours? They all look the same to me. And how do you separate them from the others?"

"Don't worry about that. Just come with me and see what happens". With that he rose and picked up his crook and started walking slowly up the hill towards the enclosure, talking to the sheep as he went. Ari was astounded to see, here and there, a sheep detach itself from the flock, and turn to follow Shemu'el towards the fold. More and more joined them, and Shemu'el stood at the entrance counting his sheep as they entered the safety of their home on the hill.

"...98, 99, 100. They are all here, and will be safe until the morning." Shemu'el exclaimed as he piled more thorn bushes in the gateway, and prepared to lie down and sleep in the entrance.

"How did you do that?" asked Ari in amazement. "They all just came when you called."

"No problem," explained his father as he wrapped himself in his cloak and lay down. "You see, my sheep know my voice."

Psalm 23 tells us that HaShem is our Shepherd, and tends us who are His sheep. Then in John chapter 10 Jesus talks about sheep and shepherds, and says that "I am the good shepherd; I know my sheep and my sheep know me." If we are to follow Jesus as He would wish then we need to get to know what his voice sounds like, so that when He speaks we will know to whom we are listening. We do that by reading His Word, and by listening to Him. Prayer is not just talking to God and asking Him for things, but it also involves listening—who are we to do all the talking? He will talk to us, and tell us what to do, if only we give Him a chance to do so. Jesus said that He only did what His Father told him to do, and we should be trying to do the same.

PRESSED DOWN AND RUNNING OVER

The olives were ready to harvest, but what was he to do?

Yosef folded his hands on the top of the gate and contemplated the dusty road that passed by, and thought hard. Behind him the gnarled olive trees in his grove were heavy with ripe fruit, their branches bowed down, ready to be relieved of their burden.

The fruit was ready to be picked, but who could Yosef get to do the work? All the village men were either away with their flocks and herds, or busy with their own pursuits, and he had no labor.

Voices reached his ears, and he looked up to see three young boys on their way home from the rabbi's house after their morning's schooling. Ari and his friends Ezra and Matthias were grumbling as they scuffed their way along the road;

"I think we are getting too old to play games with the children these days. When I have finished my chores at home I want to do man stuff."

"Yeah, me too!" They smiled and waved at the kindly owner of the olive grove as they passed him.

"Hmm," Yosef thought. "That might work."

Next morning he dressed carefully and set out to make some calls in the village.

Myriam was sweeping the dust from her house when a shadow fell across her doorway. She looked up to see Yosef standing nearby.

"Oh!" she exclaimed, "You scared me for a moment. Can I help you?"

"I will not come in while your husband is away, but I need to talk to you. May we sit out here?" He motioned to a bench outside the door. Myriam bowed her head, murmured

"I'll bring cool water," and turned away.

A few moments later she returned bearing two goblets brimming with water, handed one to Yosef and sat down at the other end of the bench. They chatted for a while and then Yosef came to the point of his visit.

"My olives are ready to be harvested, and all the men are otherwise occupied. Do you think perhaps Ari and his friends would be interested in helping me? They are growing up now and perhaps are ready to take on more responsibility."

Myriam pondered this for a while. "It may be so," she answered. "They all have chores to do at home, but that does not take up all their time, and I notice they sometimes stand around watching the little ones play, without joining them. Let me talk to Ari and I will let you know what he says."

"I'll come back tomorrow for his answer." Yosef finished his water, set down the goblet beside him and stood up. "Thank you for the water. Now I must go and talk to Ezra's mother, and Matthias' aunt."

When Ari got home from school that afternoon Myriam gave him a meal of figs and honey cakes, and then said,

"Yosef from the olive orchard asked me this morning if you and your friends would like to help him with the olive harvest.

You would need to help me first and then you could go and pick olives. What do you think?" Ari's face lit up and he asked.

"Do you mean just like a real job?"

"Just like a real job." Myriam smiled. "Are you old enough to do it properly and not just play at it?"

"Oh yes, I am ready to do grown-up stuff, and so are my friends." Ari was enthusiastic about this new possibility. "I must go and talk to them about this." He ran off in the direction of Ezra's house.

The next afternoon, after Myriam and the others had confirmed to Yosef that the boys were willing to help him, the three friends met and walked together to the olive grove, giggling and cuffing each other playfully along the way. Yosef was waiting for them and explained what he expected them to do. They were to harvest the olives first of all by picking the fruit on the outside of the trees. This was the first to ripen because it received the most sun. After that would come the fruit further in on the branches, and finally they would shake and possibly beat the trees with poles to make the olives drop onto mats laid on the ground. Then they would gather the fruit into baskets and carry it to the olive presses nearby. After that they would help with the pressing and put the precious oil into containers.

Olive oil was a very important part of the lives of the people. There were usually three pressings corresponding to the three separate harvests. The first pressing was that done in a mortar. This produced the purest oil, and was the only kind used for the lamps in the synagogue. The second pressing, done with a log, gave a good grade of oil which was used for cooking and eating, and the third and coarsest oil produced by grinding in a mill helped to fuel the cookstoves and lamps in the village houses.

The three friends set to work with a will and energetically shook the old olive trees to loosen the fruit, which dropped onto the mats underneath. This proved to be great fun, and Ari grinned at his friends happily as he swung on the branches and made them give up their heavy load.

The evening came before they had done more than a part of the orchard, but Yosef was happy with the results, and the boys promised to come again the next day to do some more harvesting.

As the days passed Ari, Ezra and Matthias became quite skilled at making sure all the fruit was off a tree before they moved on to the next one. They picked up the mats full of olives and poured the fruit into baskets and carried it to the stone press in the middle of the orchard. They enjoyed this work, as it made them feel like the men they were soon to become. Yosef worked alongside the boys, getting to know them, joking and telling them stories. He enjoyed their company, and they in turn grew to love this genial man.

The next job was to press the oil, which was hard work, but they had a donkey to help them. They put the fruit into a shallow rock cistern, and crushed it by means of a vertical millstone with a hole in it to take a pole, which was pushed round and round by two men, or in this case, a donkey and a couple of boys. The oil that resulted came out of two holes near the base of the cistern, and was carefully gathered into jars which Yosef put ready. Ari was surprised to see Yosef blindfold the donkey the first time they used the press.

HELEN THORNTON

OLIVE PRESSING

"Why do you do that?" he asked. "The poor animal cannot see where he is going."

Yosef explained, "He does not need to see where he is going. He walks round in a circle and this is to stop him getting dizzy."

By this time several weeks had passed, and the three workers were tired, but they had promised to help Yosef with the olive harvest, and they were responsible enough to see the job through to completion. They dragged their feet on the way home, and Matthias exclaimed

"I will be glad to see this finished; it has been a lot of hard work, but it makes me feel good to do this for Yosef." Ari agreed, and suggested that maybe they were ready to play games again for a while, and then perhaps they would be able to find something else to do in their spare time. Somebody, somewhere, would need them to help in some way.

THEY CALLED HIM RABBONI

On the last day, when all the oil was safely in jars and put into storage, Yosef thanked Ari, Matthias and Ezra for all their hard work, and gave them each a big jar of oil to take home. This would be used in their homes during the coming winter, for many uses, and would be a big help for their families. Yosef waved to them as they set off down the road, carefully carrying their brimming jars of oil, and called after them,

"See you next year." They agreed that it really had been a lot of fun, and next year they would be even bigger and stronger.

Scripture tells us in Luke 6:38 to "Give, and it will be given to you. A good measure, pressed down, shaken together and running over, will be poured into your lap." As Ari, Ezra and Matthias gave their time to Yosef, they were repaid, not only with a good measure of oil, but also in their knowledge of themselves and what they were capable of doing, and this made them feel good.

IN MY FATHER'S HOUSE

Sarah was so excited! There was going to be a wedding in the village.

Her great friend Leah was to become betrothed to Gideon, Sarah's cousin, the son of Myriam's older brother, and she was to be the chief attendant at the wedding.

Gideon lived with his parents, Binyamin and Rivqah, in a nearby village. He and his father were fishermen, and spent their time in small boats netting fish for a living. The young couple did not really know each other, but they had met when Binyamin and his family came to visit Shemu'el and Myriam. Leah knew that Gideon was tall, with a dark beard, and she had been drawn to him when they met.

For his part, Gideon felt that Leah was pretty, and he had heard that she was hard-working. She was the right age for him; a few years younger, and he believed she would make him a good wife, so he went to his father and asked him if he was willing to approach Leah's parents on his behalf.

So one day a procession came from Binyamin's village. He and Gideon with a few chosen friends paid a formal call on Leah's parents. They discussed the dowry, the price that Gideon would pay for his bride, and when they had agreed on the right amount a solemn marriage covenant was established.

A cup of wine was shared, and Gideon and Leah were now regarded as husband and wife. Before he could take her home, however, a great deal had to happen, and a year would pass before they would start their new life together.

Leah would now have to wear a veil over her face when she appeared in public, to show that she was promised in marriage and other men should not look at her. She and Sarah and her other attendants would spend the time in gathering her trousseau and preparing for married life.

Gideon returned home with his father, and went back to work. He would not see Leah for a year, but would spend his time in preparing a place for her to live. It was customary for the groom to build a room onto his father's house for his bride.

Sarah chattered away as the family gathered that evening, describing the activities of the betrothal ceremony.

"I can't wait for all this to start," she bubbled with excitement. "Leah and I have so much to do in the next few months."

Ari sniffed at his sister's enthusiasm. He was disgusted with the whole idea of the wedding, and did not want to get involved. He had much better things to do with his time, like practising with his sling, and hanging out with Ezra and Matthias, his friends.

Several months passed. Sarah spent much of her time with Leah, helping her with her wedding preparations, giggling with her friend, dreaming and wondering what married life would really be like.

"I hope that my parents will find a husband for me before long. I can't wait for my turn to be a bride."

"Don't be in too much hurry," cautioned Leah's mother. "Childhood is so precious, and once you are married you will take on a whole new set of responsibilities. Leah is a couple of years older than you, and she is ready for this. You are still young; hold onto your youth for a while longer." She laid aside her sewing. "I must go and prepare our evening meal. Dan'yyel and our son will be home soon, and they will be hungry."

Ari meanwhile went about his own concerns, not interested in the wedding. He and the other boys sometimes went to visit Yosef, the kindly owner of the olive grove, listening to his stories and doing odd jobs for him like sweeping out his courtyard and picking up fallen twigs and branches.

One day Myriam asked Ari to take a parcel to her nephew Gideon.

"He will need this. It is a mat that I have made for the new room he is building for his bride." Ari collected his two friends and they set out for the nearby village. On reaching his uncle's house he found the men were not there.

"They are down on the shore." Rivqah told them. "They have been fishing, but should be almost done by now."

The boys wandered down to the lake, and found Binyamin and Gideon had just finished unloading their catch, and were preparing to mend the holes that the fish had torn in their nets.

"Sit down and chat while we work," they said, "or maybe you can help us." Binyamin passed Ari a hank of the rope that they used for their nets, and demonstrated the complicated knots that they used to mend the holes.

"You had a good catch today." Matthias commented.

"Yes," Gideon replied. "It will help to pay for some of the materials that I need to complete my building project."

"How is it going?" Ari wondered.

"Not too well," Gideon replied. "It is slow work, and I am anxious to get it finished so that I can go and fetch Leah. I cannot get married properly until I have a home for her, and my father tells me that it is done to his satisfaction." Gideon looked glum, and then his face brightened. "Hey, how about you three giving me a hand with the building!"

Ari, Ezra and Matthias looked at each other.

"That might be fun," they allowed. "What would we have to do?"

"Well, I usually work on it in the afternoons, because we need to fish in the mornings. The walls are mostly done, but the roof is still not finished, and there are a lot of other small jobs that need to be completed. If you can spare the time come on over and I'll put you to work."

It was agreed that they would help, and later that afternoon Ari found himself working with ropes as he tied down the rafters on top of the new room at Binyamin's house. The three friends spent many afternoons with Gideon thereafter, working on the new house, learning new skills, and enjoying their time together, with a purpose to fulfill.

The house was finally completed, and Binyamin gave his approval. It was time for Gideon to fetch his bride. Sarah reported that Leah was ready too, and the year of waiting had just about come to an end. Leah would not know when her bridegroom would come, but it would probably be at night, and she would not have much notice, so she would need to be packed and ready to leave at any time. She would have Sarah and her other attendants with her and their lamps would need a plentiful supply of oil.

Gideon had asked Ari, Ezra and Matthias to be part of his wedding party, and one day soon the message came. This was the night. The boys already knew where they were to meet Gideon to start the torchlight procession, and they had their torches ready. These consisted of poles with old rags tied on one end, and dipped in olive oil, ready for lighting when the time came.

After dark, the men and boys met at the agreed time and place, lit their torches and walked together to Leah's house to fetch the bride. They gave a great shout and blew their shofars loudly to alert her that they were coming, so she would be ready with Sarah and the others to meet them with their lamps lit. Leah was gently lifted and placed in a specially decorated carrying chair for her journey to her new home, and the triumphal procession set out for Gideon's village. She was veiled, and would remain so until the next day.

When they reached Gideon's home they found many wedding guests there, and a great feast which Rivqah, Myriam and their helpers had prepared. A special canopy was ready for the bridal couple; they recited seven blessings and shared a cup of wine. Gideon took Leah to the new room to live with him as his wife, and the guests continued the wedding feast and made merry with singing and dancing for the next seven days. This was a time to celebrate.

Ari was exhausted after all this, but exhilarated too. He had learned new skills and had gained more knowledge of what life was going to be like. One day it would be his turn to build a room onto Shemu'el's house for his bride, but he was in no hurry. That day would come, all in good time.

John 14:2-3 tells us, "In my Father's house are many rooms…I go there to prepare a place for you…that you also may be where I am." After His resurrection Jesus returned to heaven to prepare a room—a mansion, a dwelling place—for his Bride, and He will return one day to take us, His Bride, back to live with Him forever. We do not know when that will be, but the Father will name the date, all in His good time.

GRAFTED IN

Myriam and Sarah busied themselves cooking and packing for their trip. The younger children were underfoot, as such children tend to be, vying for their mother's attention.

Myriam called to Ari, "Please take the little ones into the other room and keep them occupied for a while. I cannot work with them here just now."

They all planned to attend an extended family gathering in a nearby village, where Shemu'el's sister Rachel lived with her husband and children. Natan was a well-to-do farmer, whose property included a vineyard.

The grape harvest was ready, and every year at this time the extended family gathered to help pick the grapes and press them. Natan was locally famous for his wine, and this year the harvest was plentiful.

So Myriam and all the children planned to leave the next morning. Ari and the adults could cover the distance in half a day, but the little ones, Dawid, Lydia and the youngest, Yoel, would need to be helped and even carried part of the way. Shemu'el would join them when he could leave the sheep he was attending.

Early in the morning Ari saddled up the donkey they had borrowed from Yosef at the olive grove. Yoel was seated on its back and all the food and clothing they would need for the next few days was packed into various bags on the patient animal's sides.

The little procession set off; Ari leading the donkey with Yoel, Dawid and Lydia all over the place, in front, behind, and in the middle, and Sarah and her mother brought up the rear. It was hot and dusty, and before long Lydia was just plodding along, periodically wailing,

"Are we there yet?"

After a couple of hours Lydia just plonked herself down on her fat little bottom on the dusty path and announced,

"Tired! Carry!"

The Pool

Myriam pleaded with her daughter, "Just a little farther, please, we are nearly at a place where we can stop and rest." Around the next corner they came to a place where the stream they had been following widened into a pool, surrounded by shady trees. They stopped thankfully, dropped their loads, and waded into the shallows to cool their tired feet. They sat down and rested for a while, and ate some figs and almonds before continuing on their way, refreshed.

When they finally reached Natan's farm, there was a joyful reunion. Weariness forgotten, the children ran off to play with their cousins, while the womenfolk started laying food out on the tables that had been prepared. Ari unloaded the donkey and turned the tired beast into the pasture with Natan's animals for a well-deserved rest, then wandered off with his uncle to have a look at the farm. Much of the vineyard was planted with mature vines, on which the ripe fruit was hanging in great bunches, but there was a part of the vineyard where the only plants looked like rows of dry sticks.

Ari of course was full of questions. "What are those? Why are there no leaves on them? Are they dead?"

"No," replied Natan with a smile. "That is the root stock for the next lot of vines. You see, one kind of grape has sturdy roots that go down deep into the fertile soil, but that kind does not produce fruit that is good for wine. There are other kinds that produce wonderful fruit, but their roots are rather weak, so we have found a way to combine the two kinds of vine, and that is called 'grafting', so that the good roots are able to feed the branches that bear good fruit. Come back in the spring and I'll show you what we do. In the meantime we have a feast to eat and a harvest to reap. Let's go!"

The next couple of days were busy. Natan and one of his men were the first to go through the vineyard, They carried big knives, and inspected each vine, cutting off all the branches which did not bear fruit, and stacking these branches in great piles to be burned later. Then all except the smallest children spent their time picking big luscious bunches of grapes, sneaking a few to eat, and carrying the rest in baskets to the wine press, where the grapes were trampled underfoot. Streams of juice were caught in huge jars, to be turned into wine. This wine press consisted of a large cistern with holes in the bottom where the juice ran into a lower cistern and thence through spouts into the waiting jars. There were large beams fixed overhead, with ropes dangling from them, and the men trampling the grapes would hang onto these ropes to keep their balance. However, Natan always had time for fun, and set up a container where the children could press some of the grapes, and all the young people had a great time trampling the grapes, the way the men were doing it at the big wine press. Everybody's feet were stained bright purple from the grape juice, and there was much shouting and laughter as they pressed the grapes the old way.

When all the grapes were picked Ari's family started preparing for their walk home. The donkey was loaded, and as they set off, Natan reminded his nephew, "Don't forget to come back in a few months for the grafting."

"I'll be here all right," Ari promised. "I want to see how two branches can be made into one."

The months passed, and spring came at last. Ari prepared to return to Natan's farm to watch the grafting. He got there just as Natan was laying out bundles of shoots which they would graft into the root stock to produce good fruit-bearing vines.

With a sharp knife, Natan cut off the root stock about two feet from the ground. Then he cut a cleft in the top of the stock, and inserted two shoots into the cleft after cutting their bottom edges into a wedge, so they would fit. Then he tied it all together with a fine rope so that the shoots would stay in place. After showing Ari how to do this he handed him a knife and told him,

"Your turn now. You have seen how to do this grafting, so you try." Ari took the knife with some trepidation. He was not sure he could do this. But Natan encouraged him, saying that he would never learn to do anything just by watching someone else; he had to try it for himself. It took Ari a few tentative tries to cut the cleft in the top of the rootstock, to make it deep enough without damaging it. When he had inserted the shoots and tied it all together he stepped back with a grin. He had done it. His uncle clapped him on the shoulder and said,

"Well done! You will make a fine farmer one day if you keep on this way." Ari was pleased to have accomplished something to make Natan happy, and the two of them worked together in harmony for the rest of the day.

In a few weeks they would be able to remove the binding, and see how parts of two different plants had become one, the shoot now budding, being fed by the strong root stock, and the whole plant on its way to becoming what it was meant to be, a vibrant vine with the potential for producing good fruit which would be used to feed the people of the village.

Ari pondered all this on his way home a few days later. He was not sure that he really wanted to be a farmer. He had helped in an olive grove, and now a vineyard, tended sheep with his father, and had seen how the fishermen threw and then mended their nets. But there were still many things he wanted to explore before he decided just what he wanted to do when he set out to make his own living.

In John 15 Jesus says, "I am the true vine, and my Father is the gardener. He cuts off any branch in me that bears no fruit…I am the vine; you are the branches. If a man remains in me and I in him, he will bear much fruit; apart from me you can do nothing…" He was talking to the Jews of His day, but also to us. Unless we are grafted into the true vine we will not be able to produce the fruit that He has designed us to do, and if we are not fruitful we will be cut off and thrown into the fire to be burned.

This does not mean that we have to keep on 'doing' in order for God to love us. He loves us no matter what; we just have to believe in Him, but He also expects us to produce good fruit, even if it is just in ourselves, growing every day to be more like Him.

ARI'S SPECIAL DAY

Ari was all excited when he woke up that morning. Today he would legally become a man. He had celebrated his thirteenth birthday a few days ago, and today was the first Shabbat after that date. This morning when the family went to the synagogue he would become Bar Mitzvah, literally 'son of the covenant'.

Becoming Bar Mitzvah was a great occasion for Jewish boys. There was no big celebration or ritual involved, but as from today he was now considered old enough to bear responsibility for his own actions, good or bad. He was also old enough to be part of a minyan, that special group of ten Jewish men who would constitute a necessary minimum for a service at the synagogue, and could be called up to read from the Torah. Also, and this he considered funny, he was now legally old enough to marry, but that event was in the far distant future so far as he was concerned! There was too much to live and to learn before he would be ready for that kind of commitment. Why, he did not know any girls in the village with whom he would consider spending time these days, let alone marry!

He stretched a few times and rose from his sleeping mat. Shemu'el was home for a couple of days for the occasion, and Myriam had prepared a special breakfast for him this morning before they went to the synagogue. Ari nudged his brother Dawid gently with his foot, to wake him up.

"Come on, sleepyhead," He told him. "Time to get moving. We have things to do." Dawid groaned, but obediently opened his eyes.

Ari carefully attached his new tefillin; the scriptures a man wears on his left arm and forehead. He had been practicing this for a couple of weeks, adjusting the straps which were wound around his arm and head. Shemu'el checked him out and complimented him on doing it correctly. After eating their morning meal the family set out on foot for the synagogue. Shemu'el carried a small parcel, but refused to be drawn on the subject of its contents.

When they reached the synagogue they found Ari's friends waiting for him, along with Rabbi Moshe. Matthias was already Bar Mitzvah, but Ezra was a couple of months younger, so his time had not yet come.

"Shabbat Shalom," Rabbi Moshe greeted them. "Shalom aleichem, Ari. Are you ready to make aliyah this morning?" He reminded Ari that he would be called for the second aliyah, which meant 'to come up' to read from the Torah. Ari knew what passage he would be reading. In fact he had been trying to memorize it for the last few weeks, but was not at all certain that he had it all off by heart. He hoped so! He would also be expected to ask a blessing over the Torah.

The family entered the synagogue, remembering to touch two fingers to the mezuzah on the door as they went in. The women and girls, Myriam, Sarah and Lydia went to their side, along with young Yoel, who was too young to be left with the men. Ari, Dawid and Shemu'el headed for their seats on the men's side, flanked by his two friends, with Ari accepting compliments and best wishes from those who had arrived before them.

The readings from the Torah began, and when it was Ari's turn to 'go up', he stood, and his father stood with him. He opened the parcel he had been carrying, and took out a new prayer shawl, which he carefully draped over Ari's head and shoulders. Ari glanced at Shemu'el and whispered his thanks for the special present and made his way to the front, where the Torah scroll was kept. Finding his place, he put his finger there to mark it, and started reading his assigned portion from Bereshit, or Genesis. In fact, he kept his head up and recited it from memory, feeling somewhat surprised that it came back to his mind in its entirety. He had indeed learned it well. It was not in fact a difficult passage, being the story of Ya'acov returning home with his wives and children, and spending the night wrestling with an angel. When he had finished reading, he spoke the blessing which he had also memorized, and returned to his seat. Shemu'el patted his knee as he sat down, and whispered, "You did well. I am proud of you!"

During the remainder of the day until sunset, it being Shabbat, no work was done, but there was much visiting back and forth among the houses of the village. Many people dropped in to congratulate Ari on reaching manhood, and to wish him well.

Early the next morning, Shemu'el left for the place where he had left his sheep under the care of one of his partners. Ari walked some distance along the path with his father, chatting as they went. Shemu'el was reminding Ari that he would have increased responsibilities, and joked that it was a big relief that he would no longer have to bear the burden of Ari's deeds, but that the boy would need to learn how to conduct himself without having to ask permission to do everything. He said he was not really worried though, since "your mother and I have taught you well, and you are mature for your age. You will of course continue to live at home for several years yet, but you are now supposed to have a spiritual maturity that lets you know the difference between right and wrong."

In particular Shemu'el rehearsed Ari in his part in the ritual with which the family celebrated every Friday evening at the beginning of Shabbat. Since the Jewish day began and ended at sundown, Shabbat dinner was eaten on Friday evening.

Shemu'el would be away this next week, so it would be Ari's job as the man of the family to say Kiddush. Ari assured him that he had been watching and listening carefully, and that he knew what he had to do.

They reached the point where they would part, Shemu'el to continue on to the sheep pasture, and Ari to return home. Shemu'el hugged his son and said he would see him soon. Ari promised to take good care of the family while his father was away.

Ari was thoughtful as he made his way back to the village. He had to ponder all that had happened in the last couple of days.

Friday came, Erev Shabbat, the day before Shabbat. Myriam was busy preparing for the Shabbat, since no cooking or other work could be done that day, and all meals had to be ready to eat. She carefully laid the table with the two lamps and the containers of wine. She made two loaves of the special challah bread and covered them with a clean cloth. Finally, just before sundown, a shofar blast from the synagogue warned everyone to stop work and begin to observe the Shabbat.

The family gathered round the table, Ari in his father's place as man of the house. Myriam lit two lamps, saying the traditional blessing, "Baruch ata Adonai…Blessed are You Lord our God, King of the Universe, who brings forth light out of darkness." Everyone remained standing, and there was no talking while the ritual was taking place. Ari and his mother blessed the younger children, placing hands on their heads in turn, and then he said the usual prayer for Myriam, which brought tears to her eyes. Her son was trying so hard to take his father's place this evening! It was time for the Kiddush, the prayer of sanctification of the Shabbat; "Blessed are You Lord our God, King of the Universe, who creates the fruit of the vine." Everybody took a sip of the wine, the younger children screwing up their faces as they tasted the rough brew. Ari passed round a basin of water with a towel so that everyone could wash their hands and be ceremonially clean. Again there was a blessing to be said, "Blessed are You Lord our God, King of the Universe, who has sanctified us through your commandments and instructed us concerning the washing of hands."

Finally they were able to sit, while Ari uncovered and lifted the bread. This represented the manna which had fallen in the desert, feeding the multitudes of Israelites as they were escaping from the slavery in Mitzrayim. There were always two loaves, symbolizing the fact that on Friday there was a double portion, to last through the Shabbat when no manna fell. The cover represented the dew which always covered the manna to keep it fresh until it could be gathered. He broke the bread, reciting the blessing, "Blessed are You Lord our God, King of the Universe, who brings forth bread from the earth." Each one broke a piece off and ate it.

Then the meal was served, and it was a happy family time with everyone relaxed and ready for the day of rest, Afterwards grace was said, giving thanks to HaShem for his bountiful goodness. The lamps were not extinguished, but were allowed to burn down naturally, providing light for the evening's activities. The next day would be spent quietly, with no work being done, with everyone attending the synagogue and then visiting with friends and family until Shabbat was over.

Before retiring for the night, Myriam, Sarah and Ari sat talking quietly. Myriam put an arm around Ari's shoulder, and told him, "You did well tonight, my son. You have proven that you are now a man, and are ready to take your place among the other men of the village. But I hope that you will stay with us for a long time, for we love you, and there will always be a home for you here."

―――――――――――――――――――――

To this day Jews around the world celebrate a boy becoming Bar Mitzvah, though these days the ceremony can become quite elaborate and parties are the norm. Erev Shabbat is also a weekly occasion in Jewish homes, as well as those of believers. Two candles replace the oil lamps, and they signify 'creation' and 'redemption', but otherwise the Kiddush is much the same as it was in the first century.

CHANUKAH

Myriam rummaged frantically in a basket in the store room. "Where did I put the childrens' dreidels?" she asked herself. "I was sure I had put them in this basket! Chanukah is almost here, and I am not ready!"

It was the month of Kislev, in the darkest time of the year, just before the winter solstice, and all the villagers were preparing for Chanukah, the Feast of Lights.

"Aah," she sighed as her hand closed round a knobbly bundle wrapped in a soft cloth. She straightened up thankfully, her other hand massaging her tired back. She still had so much to do. She opened the bundle and looked at the dreidels, little spinning tops with four squared sides with letters on them. The children would really enjoy playing with these during the next few days.

Myriam smiled to herself as she remembered her father telling the story of Yehudah Maccabeus as the family gathered around the fire when she was a child. Tonight they would re-enact this. Shemu'el was back from tending his sheep and the whole family was home. Tradition was strong in their culture and most families in the village would be doing the same thing. She placed the dreidels where she could easily put her hands on them and set several clay lamps at the entrance to their courtyard for later use. Across the way her friend Shoshannah was doing the same thing. The women smiled at each other and waved, and stopped for a short chat. "I really don't have time to talk right now; I still have things to do, but let's get together tomorrow and have a good talk. We have not spent time together for a while." Shoshannah smiled at her friend and turned to go back into her own house.

As it started to get dark the family gathered around the fire in the courtyard. Shemu'el had little Lydia on his lap, with his arm around her as she leant into her father, and his other arm was cuddling Dawid close to his side. Myriam had baby Yoel sleeping on her breast, while the older children, Sarah and Ari, sat on the other side of the fire.

Shemu'el started the story the way all good stories start; "Once upon a time," He said. "Once upon a time, some two hundred years ago, during the time of the Second Holy Temple, a cruel ruler of our people called Antiochus tried to force the Jews to turn away from our religion. He was a member of the Syrian-Greek regime that was in charge at that time, and he wanted all our people to become Greeks like himself. He outlawed many of our Jewish customs and was quick to put to death any who disobeyed, often with horrible torture. Many Jews did in fact agree with this, taking on Greek names and marrying those who were not of our faith.

"Now as you know, we Jews consider the pig an unclean animal. We do not use them for food or for sacrifice. One day the Greeks tried to force the Jewish people to sacrifice a pig to HaShem in the Holy of Holies!. An outraged crowd started to object, and an old man named Mattathias decided enough was enough, and started a full-scale rebellion against the evil rulers.

"Mattathias had five sons, all fighters, and when he died, his second son took over leadership of the fighters. His name was

Yehudah, and he was known as The Maccabee. They fought fiercely, for three years, even though Antiochus sent a powerful army to crush the rebellion, and finally the wonderful day came when they were victorious, and had driven the enemy right out of Judea.

"Among their other evil acts the Syrians had totally ransacked and defiled the Temple. When the believers went into Yerushalayim they found the Temple in a shambles and idols everywhere. They were horrified, but cleaned it up, cleansed it spiritually and re-dedicated it on the 25th of Kislev. When they came to light the menorah they could find only one small jar of pure oil which had not been desecrated. This was not expected to last more than one day, and it would take eight days to replenish the supply. They lit the menorah anyway with the precious oil, and to their astonishment the lamps remained lit for eight days until the new oil arrived.

"This was considered a great miracle and worthy of remembrance. That is why we tell the story today and why we celebrate Chanukah, which means 'dedication', and we call this the Festival of Lights. Your mother will now light the first lamp, and each day of the festival we will light one more lamp until there are eight burning."

Myriam took a taper, lit it from the campfire and used it to light one of the oil lamps that she had arranged at the entrance to the courtyard, where everyone who passed could see it. The family watched it burn for a while, and all understood that this light was not to be used for working, but was there just to be admired and enjoyed. She then passed several dreidels to her husband.

HELEN THORNTON

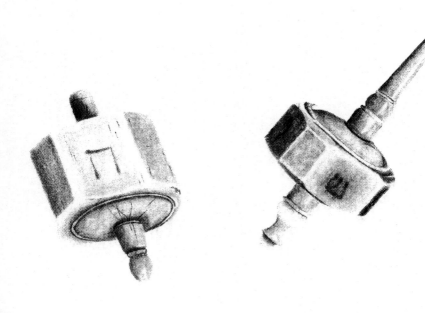

DREIDELS

"See these dreidels?" he asked. "During the Syrian reign of terror, the Jews were not permitted to study the Torah and other scrolls, but they did so anyway, and when the soldiers came around to try and catch them studying, they would tuck away the scrolls and pretend to be playing with their dreidels. See how each one has four sides, and each side has a different Hebrew letter on it. He held one up so Ari could see it. What letter is this?"

"*Nun.*" Ari answered at once.

"And this one, Sarah?"

"*Gimmel*", Sarah was able to answer correctly.

"Dawid, do you know what this third letter is?" Dawid pondered for a minute. He was just learning to read.

Then he asked hesitantly, "Is it '*Hay*'?"

"Good boy!" exclaimed his father proudly. He turned the dreidel to the fourth and last side. "How about the last letter? Anyone?"

"*Pey*" called out the two older children in unison.

"And when you put them all together what do they say?" He turned to Ari for the answer, which came immediately.

"A Great Miracle Happened Here."

"I have some very clever children," Shemu'el announced to his wife.

"Yes, so do I!" rejoined Myriam. "You have taught them well."

She stood up and started ladling their supper of thick lentil soup into bowls, while Shemu'el handed each child a dreidel and suggested they have a contest to see who could keep theirs spinning longest. "One, two, three, go!" He called. "After we eat, we'll play a game with them."

They enjoyed their evening meal of soup, with honey cakes and figs, and when all had eaten their fill, Myriam tidied away the bowls, and gave each person several raisins. "Don't eat them yet", she cautioned. "We will use them for our game." Then each person put a few in a pot in the centre, the same number for each, and took turns spinning the dreidel. Depending on what letter on the dreidel faced up when it stopped spinning, the following took place:

Nun—nothing happened, and the next player spun the dreidel.

Gimmel—the spinner took the whole pot.

Hey—the spinner took half the pot, and

Pey—the spinner had to match the pot and put into it the number of raisins that were already there.

Yoel slept peacefully as the others played for a while, as the fire died down, until two things happened; the oil lamp ran out of fuel and became dark, and Dawid got wildly excited when he spun a gimmel and won the pot. He crammed all the raisins into his mouth and chewed them while his mother announced that it was "Bedtime for you my boy; you have had enough for one day," and led him off to his sleeping mat. The others chatted quietly for a while and then decided that it was time for them to turn in as well. Tomorrow would come soon enough, and there would be two lamps to light that evening.

From that time on, Jewish people all over the world have observed a holiday for eight days to celebrate the historic victory over the oppressors, and the miracle of the oil, when one day's supply lasted for eight days. Outside of Israel, the fourth letter on the dreidel is '*shin*', which makes the sentence read "A Great Miracle Happened There" instead of 'Here'.

The candelabra, with nine candles, is called a 'chanukiah'. One, the most prominent candle is called the 'servant candle' and is used to light the others; one more each evening at sundown until all are lit on the last day. They are intended to last about 30 minutes, and the chanukiah is usually placed in a window where all who pass can see that the Festival of Lights is being celebrated.

THEY CALLED HIM RABBONI

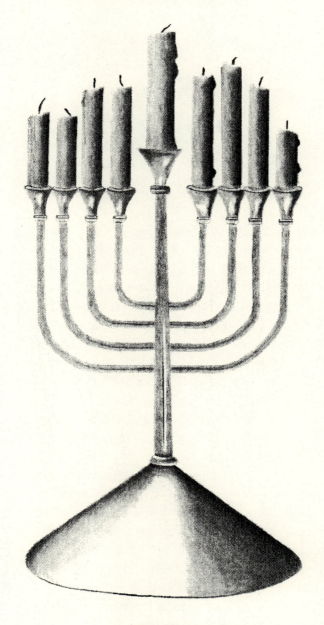

MENORAH

PESACH

Myriam and her daughter Sarah bustled around the house putting things in order. The feast of Pesach was fast approaching and they had a great deal to do in getting ready. One of their main tasks was to ensure that every scrap of leaven or yeast was out of the house. For the seven days of Pesach the family would eat unleavened bread—matzah—baked in flat squares, as any yeast was forbidden by the religious laws which they tried to keep.

They were making preparations for the big seder meal that they would share on the first day of Pesach. There would be quite a crowd, as Myriam's brother Binyamin and his wife Rivqah would be joining them, along with their neighbor Shoshannah and her family.

The younger children were outside, keeping watch for their abba who was coming home today. Shemu'el was a sheep farmer, and today was one of the busiest days of his year, as he supervised the delivery of many lambs to the market in preparation for the feast day.

Dawid came running in, followed by Lydia shouting, "Abba is coming. I see him down the road." Yoel, the toddler, was trying hard to keep up with his elders, but his fat little legs couldn't make it. He tripped and fell, crying out as he did so. Before Myriam could reach him, Shemu'el stepped through the courtyard gate, tucked the lamb he was carrying under one arm and scooped up his youngest son with the other. Yoel threw his arms round his father's neck and snuggled in, while Dawid and Lydia grabbed any part of him that they could reach, yelling with glee at being reunited with their abba.

Shemu'el grinned at his wife over the boisterous welcome of the children, and when he could move, he kissed her soundly. Then he set Yoel on the ground and hugged Sarah, dropping a kiss on her head.

"Where's my yeled, my boy? Where's Ari?" he asked.

"He's out with his friends," Myriam replied. "I thought perhaps you would have seen him down at the market. They were going down there to watch all the excitement."

Shemu'el shook his head, "No."

"He should be home in a few minutes", she continued. "He is so looking forward to seeing you again. Welcome home! It is really good to see you."

Ari wandered in soon after, his eyes lighting up when he saw his beloved abba, home before him.

"I looked for you down at the market." He told his father. "But they told me you had been and left already."

"Yes," Shemu'el answered. "I got everything done with no problems, so I was able to get home a little earlier than I had planned, and I have time to spend with my family as a result."

The evening passed quickly, with Shemu'el and the family catching up with each other's news. Bedtime came promptly, especially for the younger members, as the next day would be a busy one, and an early start was essential.

Right after their morning meal on the feast day, all the older members of the family started to fulfill their duties regarding that evening's feast. Shemu'el prepared the lamb for roasting, and then started the cooking process. Sarah was given the task of arranging the seder plate, which would be the central focus of their meal. Ari swept the courtyard and tidied it, and Myriam set about getting the remainder of the meal ready.

Sarah had six items to prepare. Each had significance. Charoset was a mixture of chopped apples, wine and spices, which brought to mind the mortar which the Israelites had used in their building projects for the Mitzrim. There was a roasted egg, which symbolized Temple sacrifices. The shankbone of a lamb reminded them of the lamb that was sacrificed by each family before the Israelites left Mitzrayim. Bitter herbs—maror—represented the bitter life of the Israelites under the Mitzrim. Finally parsley, with a bowl of salt water for dipping it, was a vegetable recalling tears. All this was set on a large clay platter in the middle of the table, and all except the egg and the shankbone would be consumed during the meal. Alongside this would be placed three matzot in a pile, separated by cloths.

The appetizing smell of roasting meat kept all the children close to home, and they played as quietly and contendedly as they could, knowing that the adults were busy. Only occasional cries of "When will dinner be ready?" punctuated the peaceful scene.

Binymin and Rivqah arrived, bearing their contributions to the feast, which included a goatskin of good red wine. Their son Gideon and his bride Leah, Sarah's friend, would be spending the day with Leah's family elsewhere in the village. The wine would be used for the four 'cups' which everyone would drink: the Cups of Sanctification, Plagues, Redemption and finally, Praise and Thanksgiving. Even the youngest child would have a tiny sip of the fruit of the vine.

Finally, Shoshanna, Aharon and their family came across the street bearing huge platters of cooked vegetables, and exclaiming that the smell of roasting lamb that had reached their house meant that they could not stay away any longer. Young Ephraim shyly handed a package to Myriam; the matzot which they had promised to provide.

Dinner was ready. This was a meal in which ceremony would play a large part. The whole thing was a re-telling of the Pesach—when the Israelites finally were allowed to leave Mitzrayim after the angel of death had visited the Mitzrim families and taken their firstborn. The Israelite families had carefully smeared the blood of their lambs on the doorposts of their houses as a sign to the angel that they were not Mitzrim, the angel had passed over these houses, and their firstborn were spared.

As the head of the host family, Shemu'el took the lead in the ritual, although Binyamin was a few years older than he. As the group gathered around the table, Myriam lit the candles with a blessing and then the first Cup was drunk with Shemu'el's reminder that they too must come out from those who are of the world and be separate unto HaShem.

The evening continued with the washing of hands and eating of the parsley dipped in salt. Shemu'el then took the middle matzah of the three wrapped in cloth, broke it in two, wrapped it again and hid half while the children closed their eyes.

The story of the Exodus of the Israelites was then told in some detail, with Dawid and Ephraim asking preset questions at certain points. The ten plagues were recited, the second cup drunk, and then it was time for the meal to be served.

It was a hearty and delicious meal, and a merry one, served by the women and enjoyed by all. The roast lamb was pronounced most excellent and the rest delectable. When the children had finished eating they set out to find the Afikomen, the hidden matzah. Lydia was the one to find it behind a basket on a shelf, and was rewarded by a small gift, which made her very happy.

After songs of praise were sung and the third and fourth cups drunk, Dawid was sent to open the door and peer out to see if the prophet Elijah was coming. A place had been set for him at the table, and left untouched in case he arrived.

"I don't see Elijah," he announced. He closed the door and returned to his seat. The prophecy was that Elijah would return before the Mashiach and announce His coming.

Shemu'el told the group that the Seder was now complete, according to custom and law, and invited them to enjoy the rest of the evening.

The adults sat around and talked for a while, as the children played quietly. Then after a while the quarreling started in the children's corner, and their parents realized that the little ones were overtired, and it was long past their bedtime. Aharon and Shoshanna scooped up their offspring, retrieved their empty platters and, making their farewells, walked back across the street to their own home. Myriam put her three to bed, while Sarah and Rivqah, who was staying overnight, finished clearing the remains of dinner and tidied up. Shemu'el, Binyamin and Ari went for a short stroll.

It had been a good evening, and there were several days of Pesach still to come. Shemu'el would stay for a while before returning to his sheep, as he did not trust the hired man for too long, and wanted to relieve him so that he too could spend some time with his family during the feast days.

Since the time of Jesus, believers still celebrate Pesach, though several modifications have been made to the haggadah, or re-telling. For example, Jesus is considered the sacrificial

Lamb who was slain for our sins, and when the afikomen, the middle one of the three matzah, is broken and hidden, this is considered symbolic of Jesus' being broken and placed in the tomb, and the stripes and piercing on the matzah remind us of how our Savior was treated while on this earth before He died, was resurrected and then ascended to heaven where He lives gloriously evermore.

GONE FISHIN'

Ari and his family relaxed over the remains of their evening meal. Shemu'el sat with the youngest member, Yoel, on his lap, the toddler curled up and sucking his thumb. Lydia played contentedly on the floor with the rag doll her mother had made for her, Dawid studied a model he was whittling, while Ari and Sarah, the teenagers, sat talking with their parents.

Ari stretched out his legs, which were growing long, and reached for an orange. He peeled it leisurely as he spoke.

"I've been thinking," he said. "I really need to consider what I want to do with my life. I am almost fifteen now." Myriam glanced over at her husband.

"We have been thinking about that too," she replied.

Shemu'el entered the conversation. "You do have a few alternatives," he suggested, "but in a small village like this one there really is not a great deal of choice."

"There are times when I would like to become a shepherd, like you," Ari nodded to his father, "but I would not want to have to spend so much time away from home." Shemu'el grimaced. He too would rather be at home more with his family, but could not afford a full-time assistant, and anyway he believed passionately that it was best for all concerned if it was the owner who tended the sheep, and not a hired hand.

Myriam got to her feet and started clearing away the dinner dishes, scraping the fish bones into a bowl to grind into fertilizer. Sarah picked up her sewing; she was making items for her future home, now that she was almost old enough to think about marrying, if only her father would find a husband for her!

"I have spent time working in an olive grove," Ari went on, "and while it was fun, I am not sure that is what I want to do all the time. I also worked with my Uncle Natan in his vineyard, but I don't think I am cut out to be a farmer of any sort. What I would really like to do for a while at least, is to go fishing. Your brother Binyamin is a fisherman," he reminded his mother, "and he and Gideon make a good living."

"It is a hard life though," Myriam replied, "and a dangerous one. The wind out on that lake can be vicious, and it can get up so suddenly."

"I realize that, but one cannot avoid danger all one's life, and I have thoroughly enjoyed being out on the lake the few times I have been able to go out in the boat. I would like at least to talk to my uncle and see whether he will let me spend some time with him out there, see whether I think it is for me or not."

Shemu'el and Myriam had no real objection to this, so it was arranged that Ari would go and see his uncle and see what could be worked out.

Ari set off the next day for the nearby fishing village where Myriam's brother lived and worked. He called in at the house first to greet his aunt Rivqah, and she told him that Binyamin and Gideon were probably down on the beach mending their nets after their night's fishing. He found them there and they welcomed him and invited him to sit down. Then they handed him a net and a needle and suggested he help them. This gave him the opening he wanted and he started in with his request.

"I was wondering if it would be possible for me to spend a few weeks out on the boat with you. I need to find an occupation for myself, and don't think I am called to be a farmer or a shepherd like Abba. What do you think?"

Binyamin pondered this for a moment. "Yes, I think that would work. One of my men, Eli, wants some time off to visit his family in Natzarat. His daughter is expecting her first child, and he would like to be there to support her. So if you can be here two days from now, you could come out with us. We will be leaving in the late evening to spend the night fishing. Would that suit you? If so, I can let Eli know that he can go to his family with my blessing."

Gideon spoke up. "Perhaps Sarah would like to come with you to spend some time with my Leah. She too is expecting, and would probably love to have her friend here for a while to keep her company." Ari thought that was a great idea, and resolved to bring his sister with him when he returned.

So two days later Ari and Sarah, carrying a few belongings, walked to the fishing village. Sarah had a happy reunion with her friend Leah, and Ari sought out Binyamin and Gideon to prepare for the night's fishing. He had a good look at their boat, so as to become more familiar with its various aspects. It was a simple wooden boat, built mainly of cedar and oak, about 26 feet long, and 7 feet wide, which would accommodate five men and their catch of fish. There was a simple sail, and oars to help propel the craft in the event that there was no wind. The nets they would use were carefully stowed in the stern, in such a way that it would be easy to spread them as they were thrown. There were few comforts, just wooden benches to sit on—not that there would be much time for sitting, they hoped! The boat was drawn up on the beach, where it would be pushed off into the water when it was time to go.

After an evening meal which Rivqah prepared for them, the men gathered for their night's work. Binyamin introduced Ari to his helpers, Dan and Kalev, telling them that his nephew would be joining them for a time, while Eli was away. They studied him with some suspicion; a slight youth, but realized that he was wiry and strong, and would probably be able to pull his weight, and that therefore they would not need to baby and protect him after all. They hoped so, anyway.

There was a great bustle on the waterfront as the fishing fleet prepared to get under way. Men called across the water to friends on other boats, with a good deal of good-natured banter. Zebediah owned several boats, which were manned by hired hands, since his sons had gone to be with Yeshua. Ya'aqov and Yochanon were two of the Teacher's closest companions. Zebediah missed them, but they did get home once in a while, and he understood their need to be with Yeshua at this time.

FISHING BOATS

Ari looked around him, drinking in the scene with some bewilderment. There were so many new things for him to learn.

Binyamin beckoned him over. "Just watch us tonight, and try to remember how things are done. If we need you to do anything we will let you know." Ari climbed aboard and sat down in the bow, where he thought he would be out of the way. Gideon made sure everything was in order, and then stationed himself at the tiller. Kalev picked up several palm branches from a pile on the beach, and deposited them on the boat next to Ari.

"What are those for?" Ari asked him.

"I don't have time to explain now, but you will see later," was the brusque reply.

With Binyamin, Gideon and Ari on board, Dan and Kalev started pushing the boat into the water until she floated; then scrambled aboard and picked up the oars to get her out into deeper water. After a short while Binyamin gave the signal to hoist the sail, the wind filled it and they began to move swiftly towards the fishing grounds. All around them the fishing fleet kept pace, and the shouting between boats continued with much hilarity.

They reached the place where the men reckoned the fish would be, though to Ari one spot looked exactly like another. He was going to ask questions, but there was a sudden cessation of talk as they hauled down the sail and got down to business, so Ari decided to save his questions for later. Gideon and Dan picked up the net, handling it carefully so as not to tangle it, and at a signal, threw it over the side in such a way that it spread out to form a circle some twenty feet across. The edge of the net was weighed down with sinkers so that as it fell through the water it trapped the fish beneath it.

Kalev picked up the palm branches and handed one to Ari. "What we do with these is scare the fish into the net by beating the water with branches." Ari thought this sounded a bit weird, but dutifully beat the top of the water, and when he glanced at the other boats he saw they were all doing the same thing. When it seemed that the net was sufficiently full, they all started hauling on the ropes that closed the net, calling on Ari to do his part. The net grew heavier and heavier, and when it got close they could see a great many small fish thrashing around inside it. It took the combined efforts of three men to drag the net over the gunwale and empty it into the bottom of the boat.

"Catching these tiny fish is a mixed blessing," Gideon explained to Ari. "We can sell them to the fish processors, but they don't give us very much for them. What is good about catching them though is that they feed heavily on the plankton and don't leave much for the bigger fish. So with fewer of these there is more food for the fish we need to catch and sell."

By now it was almost midnight, and they stopped work for a while to eat what they had brought with them. It was good to sit down for a while, though they were ankle deep in still-flopping fish. After a short rest Binyamin gave orders to hoist the sail again, saying they were going elsewhere to look for larger fish.

After casting their net a few more times there were enough fish in the boat for the tired men to hoist the sail and head for home. The fish buyers from Migdala were waiting for them and helped haul the heavy boats up the beach.

Their work was not yet done though. Ari, Gideon and the men had to disentangle some of the fish from the net, and inevitably holes were torn in the fabric. Binyamin as the owner of the enterprise dealt with the buyers, selling most of the larger fish, but keeping a few choice ones for the family. The small fish were sold for their oil. When all had been unloaded, the men sat down on the beach to mend the nets, which was a chore that had to be done every day. The nets were then dried and folded and stored, ready for the next trip.

As they trudged home for a few hours sleep, Ari started asking his uncle questions.

"How do you know where to find the fish?" Binyamin answered that they found their way round the lake by lining up landmarks on the shore. The lake was only about seven miles across and fifteen long, so the land was always in sight.

"So," he asked his nephew as they reached the house where Rivqah was waiting for them with a hot meal, "Did you enjoy your first night's fishing? At least the weather was good and we did not have a gale to contend with. Sometimes we get caught by a sudden storm and then things can get really wild!" Ari was exhausted, but he nodded happily and agreed that he had had a good time, and that this was still something he wanted to try. He would finish the time he had agreed to stay and then decide if this was how he wanted to spend his days and nights for the remainder of his life.

Fishing is still a large part of the economy of the Galilee, and some of the fishermen still use the type of nets that are described in this story. Several years ago a two thousand year old boat was unearthed from the mud, and this is believed to be the kind of boat that was used by Peter and his crew. It has been carefully preserved and can be seen in a special museum in Tiberias, on the shores of the Sea of Galilee.

RABBONI

ARI'S SNACK

There was a buzz in the village. Four men from the nearby fishing village were passing through on their way home, and stopped to visit with a friend. Several people were gathered around the entrance to the courtyard where they listened to the conversation, and Ari and his two friends were among them.

Ari knew one of these men slightly; Andri was a neighbour of his Uncle Binyamin's.

Everyone listened, fascinated by the stories that Philippos and Ya'aqov told about this new Teacher, whose name was Yeshua. He traveled around teaching about a new Way, and did all sorts of miracles, healing those who were sick, and explaining how promises made in the Torah and by the prophets were actually happening. He had called several men to follow him, and these four were among his regular companions.

Ari was excited by what he heard. He whispered to his friends, "I should really like to listen to this man teach."

Ezra shrugged his shoulders. He was not so sure. "I'm sure we have heard it all before—why exert yourself!"

As the meeting broke up and the visitors prepared to leave, Ari sought out Andri and asked him how he could get near Yeshua.

"We are leaving tomorrow at daybreak to join Him." Andri told him. "Why don't you come with us?" Ari was overjoyed, and they agreed to meet early next morning. Ari went off with his friends and asked them if they were coming next day. Ezra was not interested, and Matthias had to work, but Ari had a free day, and would be able to go.

He ran home to tell his parents that he would be going with Andri the next day to hear this new teacher. He did not sleep much, but was up at the crack of dawn the next morning, and ready to set out before he realized he was not the only one up and about.

He started up the road, but his mother called him back and handed him a pouch.

"Take this food," she suggested, "It could be a long day for you." Ari thanked her and went on his way.

Soon he reached the spot where he was to meet Andri and the others, and found them just arriving. He joined them and they set out together. As they walked, Ari was full of questions about this man they called the Teacher.

"Where is He now?" he asked. Andri answered that He had said He needed a time of quiet, so spent the night on Andri's brother's boat.

"My brother Shimon," Andri smiled to himself. "Yeshua calls him Kepha, because He says he is a Rock, and that on this rock of the truth He is going to build His church. I am not sure about that—a less patient man I have yet to see! But the Teacher seems to think he is someone special."

Ari found himself walking beside Yochanon, who was Ya'aqov's brother, and just a few years older than Ari himself. They came to a place where several paths met, and discovered that a whole crowd of people, men, women and children, were going in the same direction; the news about the new teacher was spreading.

ARI'S LUNCH

Before long they came to the shore where Shimon's boat was moored, and saw Yeshua just about to disembark. Ari looked carefully at Him, but did not see what was so different about him. He was just an ordinary looking man, with dark hair and the beard that all the men wore. He wore sandals on His feet, but his stride was long, and He was obviously used to walking everywhere. He greeted His companions, and Ari faded back into the crowd. He did not feel he could intrude on their private conversation.

He watched Shimon, called Kepha, for a while, and saw him as an older, burlier version of his brother Andri. He was perhaps a little rougher, but there was tenderness in his eyes as he helped Yeshua off the boat. He was obviously very fond of Him.

Yeshua and His companions led the way up a nearby hill, to a natural hollow, where the Teacher turned and began to speak to the crowd. Everyone crowded as close as they could, and a hush descended as Yeshua started teaching. He talked about the Kingdom of heaven, which was a new concept to many, saying that He Himself was The Way into that kingdom. Some of what He said did not seem to make a lot of sense to Ari and to others, as He told many stories, but did not always stop to explain what the stories meant. For example he talked about a sheep being lost, and the shepherd dropping everything to search for this sheep, and of his joy when he found it. Ari understood that all right, for Shemu'el his father was a shepherd. But just what did that have to do with the kingdom of heaven? Ari would need to puzzle that one out.

Ari watched the Teacher's face, and saw His eyes full of fire and passion. Then something caught the Teacher's attention, and he whirled and snatched up a small child who had wandered away from his enthralled parents, fallen onto a sharp rock and cut his leg. Loud cries of pain were raised. Yeshua put His hand over the cut and prayed, and the wailing stopped abruptly. There was no longer any wound on the child's leg. As He cuddled the child His face became full of love and compassion. He said that one needed to become like one of these little ones in order to enter the kingdom. That was another puzzling statement. Then He returned the child to the arms of his relieved father, who had stepped forward to claim him.

Yeshua walked over to a large tree that was growing right out of a pile of rocks. It threw an extensive shadow, and many people were taking advantage of the shade, for the sun was hot. He pointed towards the trunk of the tree, and said, "Look at this mustard tree, how big it is, and how it grew right out of the rock. Consider the determination of the little shoot that was pushing its way towards the sunlight. The mustard seed is very tiny, yet it grows into a large tree where the birds can find shelter. But it took a lot of faith and resolve for it to get to this point. You too need to develop this kind of faith and tenacity."

The long day wore on, as the crowds listened to the teaching. Then Philippos started getting restless, and finally nudged the Teacher and said,

"Master, don't you think we should let the people go so they can visit the nearby villages and find something to eat?"

"You feed them!" rejoined Yeshua.

"But we have nothing to give them. Feeding a crowd like this one would cost many days' wages." Yeshua smiled; He knew what was coming.

Andri heard this and came closer. "Just a minute; You have given me an idea." He called to Ari who was not far away. "Didn't your mother give you some food when you left this morning? Have you eaten it yet?"

"No, I still have it," answered Ari. "I have been too busy listening to think about eating. But I am getting hungry now."

"Would you be willing to share it with the Teacher?" Andri asked. Ari handed it over without another word, and Andri opened the pouch.

"We have a few little buns and a couple of small fish." Andri passed the pouch to the Teacher. Yeshua took it, looked up to heaven, gave thanks and plunged both hands into the pouch, took out bread and fish and gave it to His companions to pass out to the crowd.

Ari thought, "That's not going to go very far!" Then Yeshua took out more handfuls of food and passed it along. And He did it again—and yet again. The food just never stopped coming! Ari stood there with his chin dropped and his mouth open in awe. He had never seen anything like this before! The five little buns and two tiny fish that his mother had packed for his lunch were feeding a huge crowd of people. Ari took his share in a daze, but could hardly eat for astonishment. Several people who had brought goatskins of water shared it with those around them.

Finally everyone had food to eat, and had eaten their fill. Satisfied, they started to leave, as some had a distance to travel before they reached home. There were scraps of bread everywhere, which filled twelve baskets, but no one was left hungry.

Ari turned for home, pondering what he had experienced that day. He would never forget how his little snack was able to feed so many. He reckoned there must have been at least five thousand men on the hillside that day, not counting women and children. Would he have some stories to tell! His family and friends would be hearing about this day for a long time to come. He fell into step with his wise friend Yosef from the olive grove, and as they walked together they talked about what they had seen and heard.

Ari asked, "What did He mean when He said we had to become like little children again? That's not possible!"

Yosef answered, "I think He means that we need to regain the trust and simplicity of a child, and just take things by faith." Ari thought about that for a long time.

As they reached their village Ari found himself being hailed as a hero by several who had been on the hill that day, who had been telling the story of Ari's snack. But Ari uttered an immediate disclaimer. "I did not do anything," he said, "except make what I had available to the Teacher. He and HaShem did the rest."

Availability is more important to HaShem than is ability. If we are willing to offer Him whatever we have, however little it seems, whether it be time, talent or treasure, He will take it and do something with it—often far more than we can comprehend at the time.

TWO BY TWO

Stefanos adjusted his cloak as he walked along the dusty path. He was a little apprehensive as he did not know what to expect today. He had been summoned to meet with the Teacher and his companions.

"I have a special task that I want you to do," he was told.

Stefanos was a young man who found himself intrigued by what the Teacher said, and for the past several weeks he had been following Yeshua and his group as they moved around the Galilee, teaching and healing the sick. His adoptive father was a wealthy merchant in Jerusalem, and though he spent a lot of his time working in the shop, with Baruch's blessing he frequently took a few days to see what the Teacher was doing, and usually brought an offering to help with Yeshua's support.

Several other men joined him as he walked to the meeting place.

"I hear the Teacher wants us to do something for him."

"You too?" Stefanos replied. "I wonder what He has in mind." When they reached their goal, Stefanos was surprised to see about sixty men gathered under a shady tree surrounding Yeshua.

"There are still a few to come," he was told. "They should be here soon." Stefanos sought out Yehudah, who was the keeper of the money bag, so that he could present his offering. Yehudah acknowledged this with a grunt, and did not bother to lift his head. Stefanos spotted his cousin Natan'el, who was one of Yeshua's close companions, and went over to talk to him.

"What's up with Yehudah today?" he asked. "He's really grouchy." Natan'el suggested that maybe things were not exactly going the way Yehudah felt they should, and he probably needed to be left alone for a while.

When the last stragglers had arrived, Yeshua stood and addressed the group.

"I asked you all to come today because I want you to go out in pairs to the villages around the Galilee and tell the people about the Kingdom of God. Tell them that I am coming their way and prepare them for me. You have all spent time with me lately, and have been listening and learning. Now I want you to put what you have learned into practice. The harvest is ripe for picking, but there are never enough laborers."

Stefanos was astounded at what he heard.

"I'll never be able to do stuff like healing the sick!" he informed Natan'el.

"Oh yes, you will," replied his cousin. "All you need is faith! The Teacher told us recently that if we had sufficient faith these mountains around us would find themselves in the middle of the Great Sea. And you know what He says about the mustard seed!"

GOING OUT TWO BY TWO

The Teacher continued with his instructions:

"I don't want you to take any provisions with you, or any extra clothing. You will be looked after by the people with whom you stay in the villages. Just be sure to stay in one house only in each village, and don't keep moving around." He had other instructions for them and they had to make sure they would remember what He said. Then He started pairing them off.

"Yitz'haq, you go with Yaa'cov, and Mattithayu with Eli." When he came to Stefanos, he paired him with Natan'el, which was a great relief to the young man. Stefanos had a lot of respect and admiration for his older cousin, who was one of the first companions to be chosen by the Teacher, and was also one of the first people to confess that he believed Yeshua was in fact the son of HaShem.

The two men took leave of the others and set out for Korazin, which was their first assignment. Along the way they talked about what the Teacher had been doing, and Natan'el filled Stefanos in on some things he had missed.

"Did you hear about the time Yeshua calmed a storm?" He asked.

"No, what happened?"

"Well one day Yeshua asked Shimon to take us across the lake in his boat. He was really tired because He had been teaching all day, so He lay down to have a nap. Yochanon brought a cushion for His head, because it was not very comfortable sleeping on the bottom of the boat! While we were crossing the lake a huge storm blew up—this lake is quite famous for its sudden storms, and I am afraid that we all got a bit scared, in fact we were terrified. The wind was so strong, and the waves were really huge, breaking over the boat and threatening to swamp us. We finally decided to wake The Teacher, and asked if he was not aware that we were about to drown.

He sat up and shouted, 'Peace, be still!,' and you know what happened? The wind and the waves died down immediately. He said to us, 'Why are you afraid? Do you still have no faith?'

I must admit it made us feel a bit ashamed of ourselves. He seemed to think we should have calmed the wind ourselves instead of waking Him. That's really something!"

They reached Korazin, and chose a house to approach. They knocked, and when the owner answered, they said, as they had been taught,

"Peace to this…" But they were not allowed to finish their blessing.

"What do you want?" the man shouted. "I know who you are, you are followers of that man Yeshua. Rabble rouser! Dogs! I won't have anything to do with you lot. He shook his fist at them. Out! Out! At once!" Stefanos and Natan'el glanced at one another, turned, and left quickly. Once out on the street, they decided to shake off the dust of that village and find another more hospitable.

Tired, and by now very hungry, they trudged towards the next village. The first house they came to was a large and clearly prosperous farm. As they greeted the owner, "Peace to this house," he smiled and invited them in.

"Sit." He commanded, and called out to his wife, "Esther, bring food, we have visitors", and to his servant, "Bring a basin of water to wash their feet. They are tired and hungry." Natan'el and Stefanos smiled gratefully at one another, and were able to relax. Maybe this assignment would not be so bad after all.

When they had satisfied their hunger, Yosef led them to secluded sleeping mats and said,

"Sleep now. We will talk in the morning." The exhausted men stopped only to offer thanks to HaShem and then fell into a deep sleep.

Awakening next morning thoroughly refreshed, Natan'el and Stefanos were soon joined by their host, who brought a basket of fruit for their breakfast. As he nibbled on a fig, he asked, "So what brought you to our village?" Stefanos was glad to explain that the man called Yeshua, whom they knew as the Teacher, had called them to go out before Him to prepare the way.

"He's coming here!" Yosef exclaimed. "Wonderful! I have been hoping to get a chance to hear Him teach, but with the farm so busy it is hard for me to get away. Let me tell my servant to spread the word around the village that you are here and Yeshua is coming."

Later the two disciples went out into the village marketplace, beside the well, where they found a number of people gathered. Some were waiting for them, and some were just fetching water or conducting their business. Natan'el started out by asking the group if they had heard about the new teachings concerning The Way. He taught for a while, and Stefanos wandered about, chatting with the children and observing the scene. They were received well, and it was obvious that what Natan'el was saying was being heard and understood. Presently Stefanos noticed one of the boys walking with a limp. He asked what was wrong, and was told that he had been kicked by a vicious goat. He took the boy's leg in his hands and asked HaShem for healing, as he had been taught. He felt heat in his hands, and when he let go of the leg he could see that it was no longer crooked, and the child was able to walk normally. Everyone could see what had taken place, and Stefanos was hailed as a healer. He was quick to say, however, that it was not he who had healed the leg, but HaShem, and He should get the praise.

A few days passed, with the two men teaching the crowds and healing the sick who were brought to them in increasing numbers. Then one day some of his neighbors brought a man to them who was clearly not in his right mind. He shouted and declaimed, and told them firmly that they had no right to be there, but that he was king of the village and anything he said was paramount. This would clearly take both Stefanos and Natan'el to deal with, so as his friends held him, they laid hands on his head, prayed out loud in the mighty Name of Yeshua, and told the demons to come out of him. He shrieked and fell on the ground and remained still. A few people rushed up, thinking he was dead, but he stirred, shook himself and stood up, looking dazed. When questioned, he gave logical answers, and it was obvious that he had been delivered of his tormentor.

That evening the man who had been healed, with his friends, gathered at Yosef's house and there was much talk of Yeshua and The Way. All came to believe in Yeshua and there was great rejoicing.

It was time for Natan'el and Stefanos to return to Yeshua, along with the others who had been sent out. Stefanos was exultant when he told the Teacher what had happened.

"Rabboni, even the demons submit to us in your Name," he reported. Yeshua smiled.

"I have given you authority to overcome all the power of the enemy; nothing will harm you. However, do not rejoice that the spirits submit to you, but rejoice that your names are written in heaven."

Stephen is not mentioned in Scripture as one of the seventy two whom Jesus sent out into the Galilee, but in order to fulfill his later position as deacon he would have had to walk with Jesus though a large part of His time of ministry, in order to gain the knowledge and maturity with which he would be credited later.

THEY CALLED HIM RABBONI

Legend says that Stephen was illegitimate, but I have portrayed him as being part of a merchant's family in Jerusalem. Baruch and his wife adopted him and loved him as their own son.

THE WOMAN FROM SAMARIA

Rivqah was a beautiful and a spirited woman. She was also a deeply unhappy one. She lived in a town in Samaria called Sychar, on the outskirts of which was found Yaa'qov's Well, situated on a plot of ground that, many years ago, the patriach Yaa'qov had bought and given to his son Yosef.

Rivqah had been the wife of Eleazar, who died, leaving her with small children. As was the custom, she approached his brother Nahum for protection. However, Nahum's wife disliked Rivqah, who was more beautiful than she was, and was jealous of her, and so made her life difficult. She was forced to return to the house of Eleazar, and although Nahum provided her with food and clothing, as was his duty, he had nothing more to do with her.

Because of her looks, and since she was a natural flirt, she had found a number of protectors since then, all of whom had left her for one reason or another. She was by no means demure, and loved to glance sideways at men, and make sure they were able to catch a glimpse of a shapely ankle, so was popular with the men of the village, but was shunned by the women, who mocked her, taunted her, and accused her of taking their husbands.

By this time her children were grown, so she was nominally acting as housekeeper to an elderly widower. But Reuven was still a virile man, and she lived with him as his wife. Even her children were ashamed of her, and had little to do with her. As a result she had no friends, was lonely, and was forced to visit the well to draw water in the heat of the day, it being too uncomfortable for her to do so in the evening as was the custom.

Meanwhile Yeshua and several of His companions were traveling from Yerushalayim to the Galilee, and He chose to go by way of Samaria. The day was hot, with the sun beating down from a cloudless sky, and the road was long and dusty. When they reached Ya'aqov's Well, Yeshua told the others, "I am going to rest here for a while. You go into Sychar and buy food for us. Meet me back here when you are done."

Yeshua's friends left Him sitting beside the well and hurried on their way to buy provisions. On the road they met Rivqah carrying her water jar. As was her flirtatious nature, she looked boldly at the men as she passed them. "Whoa," one of them exclaimed. "Did you see that? That was quite a beauty back there!"

"Come on," he was told. "She's old enough to be your mother."

"Maybe so", was the rejoinder, "but she is still one good-looker, and bold too!"

RIVQAH AT THE WELL

As Rivqah approached the well she noticed Yeshua sitting nearby, but recognized him as a Jew, and therefore unlikely to respond to her, so decided to ignore him. She set about pulling on the rope which held the leathern bucket that was used to draw water. As she poured the first bucketful into her jar a voice interrupted her.

"Do you suppose I could have a drink of that water?" Startled, she turned, to see Yeshua waiting for an answer. This was bizarre; Jewish men did not, ever, speak to Samaritan women.

"How can you, a Jew, ask me for a drink?"

Yeshua spoke again. "If you knew just who I am it would be you asking me for a drink, of living water."

She replied, with a toss of her head, "And just how do you propose to get this living water? You have no bucket, and this well is deep. Are you greater than Ya'aqov our father who gave us the well and used it himself for his family and animals?"

His reply staggered her. "Everyone who drinks from this well will be thirsty again before long. But my living water will never make you thirsty. In fact it will be like a permanent well inside you, leading to eternal life."

"I want that," Rivqah exclaimed. "I am tired of coming here every day to draw water."

Yeshua changed tactics. "Go and fetch your husband and come back."

"I have no husband," He was told.

"You are right, you have had five husbands, but your present partner is not your husband."

Rivqah was astounded. "How did you know that? You must be some sort of prophet, because nobody could have told you that about me. You Jews keep telling us that we need to go to Yerushalayim to worship, but we have always worshipped on this mountain, as our forefathers used to do."

"Listen well to what I say, woman. There will be a time coming when you will worship neither here nor there. You Samaritans do not really know whom you are worshipping. We Jews do know, because the Mashiach will be a Jew. Yet from now on true worshippers will worship in spirit and in truth, for they are the kind the Father is looking for. HaShem is spirit and we must worship Him in spirit and in truth."

Rivqah said thoughtfully, "I do know that the Mashiach is coming, and when He does, He will explain everything to us."

Yeshua replied, "You are talking to Him right now."

At this point Yeshua's companions returned from buying food, but although they were really surprised to see Him talking to the Samaritan woman, they did not feel called upon to comment. The Teacher would know very well what He was doing.

Rivqah meanwhile, forgetting her water jar, hurried back to town to tell people about this man. She shouted out to people in the streets, "Come and see a man who knows everything, even what nobody has told him. I think He is a prophet, maybe even Mashiach!" She went into the shops with the same message, and then went to Reuven's house, where she had been living, and insisted that he come with her. Many of the women brushed her off, as was their custom; she was of no account, why listen to her? But most of the men became curious, and many of them followed Reuven and Rivqah back to the well to see this man for themselves.

In the meantime Yeshua's companions had said to Him, "We brought food for you Rabboni, now you should eat something." They themselves were busily eating their own lunch. Yeshua merely glanced at them, and answered,

"Not now. I have food to eat that you do not understand."

They looked at one another, wondering. "Did someone bring him food while we were gone?"

Yeshua enlightened them, "My food is to do the will of Him Who sent Me." He went on to explain that while others had laid the groundwork, it would be up to them to reap the harvest. "Are you ready for that?" He asked.

By this time a great crowd of townspeople was surging down the dusty road, with Rivqah in the lead, dragging a reluctant Reuven by the arm. They stood around the well, or sat on the sand, waiting for Yeshua to start teaching them. This He did, talking eloquently about the Kingdom of Heaven, and of their need to repent and believe. If they would only do that they would gain eternal life. Many of them looked at each other and nodded; this was in line with what they had been taught about the coming Mashiach.

By the time evening came, it was obvious that they were not able to let the little group leave that day, and urged them to stay. Rivqah and a now-believing Reuven urged Yeshua to stay in their house, saying they would be greatly honored if the Teacher would do so. Rivqah quietly explained to her partner that she could no longer continue to live with him, but would have to return to the house that Eleazar had left her, and he agreed.

The whole group then made their way into the town of Sychar, and stayed with them for two days. Rivqah served Yeshua and His companions, but returned at night to her own house. Many of the townspeople believed, and even the women came around to the men's way of thinking, and began to realize that Rivqah had changed, and was no longer a threat to them. A few of the women even offered to help her. Rivqah accepted gratefully, friendships were formed, and a much happier Rivqah resolved that things would be different from now on.

Before Yeshua and the others left on their way into Galilee, there was a different atmosphere in the town. The people agreed that, not because of what Rivqah had told them, but because they had seen for themselves, they believed with all their hearts that Yeshua was who He said He was, the Savior of the world.

In the time of Jesus, the Jews and Samaritans were alien to one another, and had very little contact. A Jewish man would never have initiated a conversation with a Samaritan woman, but Jesus did not follow any man-made rules. He just did what His heavenly Father told Him to do, even if that flouted convention.

STORYTELLER

Yeshua was weary. He had been teaching all day, which was not unusual, but there had been some tension with his own family and he was tired. He needed to get away and talk with His Father, who would refresh and strengthen Him.

When the crowds had left for the day He told his companions to stay where they were, and wandered out of the house and down by the lake. It was cooler there, with the breeze blowing, so he sat on a rock and started to pray. Night fell, its soft darkness hiding Him from sight. Unheeding, He continued to communicate with HaShem, getting all that He needed for the next day's work.

As dawn stole softly over the lake a few early fishermen walked past, glancing at the Teacher, but not recognizing Him. He became aware of their presence, stood and stretched, but remained silent. Then others started to arrive, and these knew who He was. They left quickly and told their neighbors, "The Teacher is sitting down by the lake. Now is our chance to get near Him." Their friends spread the word, and before long he was being mobbed—again. The multitude was so large that Kepha, who had joined Him, suggested, "Why don't you climb into my boat, which is just along the beach, and teach from there? Then you will not be crowded. I'll bring it over here."

Yeshua nodded, Kepha called the other companions, who helped him maneuver his boat from where it was moored, and the Teacher climbed on board. The waiting throng thought He was leaving, and surged forward, but Kepha simply pulled out a few yards from shore and let down the anchor. Yeshua thanked him, "That was a good idea; they were getting too close, and I need some space today."

Stephanos wandered up at this point. He felt he needed to be with Rabboni for a while, but had not been sure exactly where to find Him. This was good, but what a lot of people had had the same idea! He had met with some of the women along the road and they had told him they were going to join the Master on the lakeshore. These women, who included Miriam of Magdala, and Salome, wife of Zebediah and mother of Ya'aqov and Yochanon, among others, followed Yeshua, and met his needs and those of His companions from their own resources. Stephanos was another who regularly contributed to the common purse, so he was well known to the women and to Yeshua's companions, one of whom was his cousin Natan'el. The women had brought food for Yeshua, but were distressed when they found that they could not reach Him, because of the expanse of water between them.

"Here, give me the food," suggested Stephanos. He removed his sandals, tucked up his tunic around his waist, took the basket of food and waded into the water. When he reached the boat the water was only up to his knees, but that was sufficient to deter the crowd who wanted to get close to Yeshua.

Te'oma took the basket of food from Stephanos, thanked him and the women, and passed the food to Yeshua. He paused in his teaching and slaked His thirst from the goatskin in the basket. Then He chose a small bunch of grapes and a hunk of bread spread with fresh goat cheese. The bread smelled so good, having been baked that morning in the home of Kepha's mother-in-law.

As He ate, he studied the crowd on the shore. He could see by their dress and demeanor that many of them were farmers. So He started to tell them a story.

"There was a farmer," Yeshua began, "who took his basket of barley seed and set out to plant it. As he walked through his field he took handfuls of seed from the basket and threw it out before him and to the side." The farmers in the crowd nodded; they knew and understood this. "Then he went home to wait for the harvest. But not all the seed produced fruit. Some fell on the path, and birds came and ate it. Some fell on rocky ground, and some fell in patches of thorns. The seed on rocky ground sprouted, but there was no depth of soil, so when the sun came out there were no roots and the plants died. The seed in the thorn patches also grew, but the thorns grew faster and soon choked the young plants.

"However, some of the seed fell on fertile soil and this grew and thrived. When the time came the farmer was able to reap a great harvest." The farmers agreed among themselves that this was the way of it, but that the farmer should have done a little work on the land first, removing the rocks and weeds and creating more fertile ground. Stephanos thought privately that this was a good story, but few among the crowd were able to relate it to the Kingdom of Heaven, which is what Yeshua usually talked about.

Yeshua's companions on the boat came to Him and asked, "Why do you talk in parables? Not everybody can see the meaning."

"I use parables," the Teacher answered," because most of the people I am talking to have hard hearts. They really do not want to listen to My words, but it seems for some reason to be fashionable to follow me round and listen to Me talk, but they are not going to gain anything much by doing this. They want miracles, or to get something for nothing, and some of them are even looking to hear something that they can use against Me.

"You people, however, have been given the ability to take in and profit from what I am saying, so I will tell you what this parable means."

Stephanos, who was still standing with his feet in the water, was close enough to hear this quiet exchange. He had excellent hearing, and voices carry well over water. He edged a little closer in order to catch every word.

"The parable is all about the Kingdom of God. The seed that fell on the stony soil is the people who hear the Word and accept it with joy to start with, but when the cares of this world come upon them they fall away because they have no roots. The seed that fell among thorns is the people who hear the Word and accept it, but worldly things clutch at them and in time they too fail to thrive, because the pleasures of their life become too important. The birds who eat the seed are the enemies of God's people who snatch away the teaching before it can germinate. The seed that falls on fertile soil means the people who hear the Word, take it deep into their hearts, nurture it and become fruitful, often far beyond their own expectation."

Yeshua looked up at the crowd, and noticed Yehudah at the back, taking up a collection, most of which, the Teacher knew, would end up in Yehudah's own pockets. He called out "Yehudah, I need you here with me." Yehudah's face fell; he knew he had been caught, and that he would be having a little private talk with the Teacher later, but now he obediently made his way to the front of the crowd, concealing the money bag as he went.

Yeshua continued in a quiet voice to His companions, "Now I see that the crowd is growing impatient. I had better tell them some more stories. Listen carefully for the hidden meaning. I am sure you will be able to figure it out."

Yeshua raised His voice in order that everyone could hear him. "I have another farming story for you", He announced. The crowd stopped murmuring among themselves and prepared to listen.

"The Kingdom of Heaven is like this; a farmer sowed good seed in his field, but when he turned his back, an enemy came along and threw in a lot of weeds. The farmer noticed nothing until all the seeds came up, and then it became obvious that there was an excess of weeds growing in the field. 'Who did this?' his servants asked.

'An enemy who wants to hurt me', was the farmer's reply.

'Do you want us to go and pull up all the weeds?' They asked.

'No', they were told, 'because you might pull up the good wheat at the same time. Leave it until the harvest. Then I will give orders to the harvesters to take the weeds first, and gather them in bundles to be burned, and then bring in the harvest and put it in my barns.'"

Yeshua continued to speak to the crowd, using parables, talking about such everyday things as mustard seeds, and yeast, but not offering any explanations. This crowd today was particularly hard hearted, showing little faith, and although they hoped to see miracles, there were none.

Kepha raised the anchor and they sailed away, not going far, but round the corner to the regular mooring, and Yeshua landed and went into the house. There His companions gathered round and demanded an explanation for the story about the weeds.

He sighed; when would these people start listening with their hearts? They had been with him for months, but He still had to explain everything to them in plain language.

"The Son of Man sent the good seeds—His chosen ones—into the world. The devil planted his sons, the sons of evil, among them. Then will come the harvest, the end of the age, and the harvesters, the angels, will gather up the evil doers and throw them into the fiery furnace, while the righteous will prevail, and enter the kingdom of their Father. Take note of this."

After telling them several more stories, He moved on from there to Natzarat, his home town, where once again He encountered a degree of unbelief, because the townspeople thought that they knew him as a local boy, and that therefore he could know nothing. No miracles were possible there because of their lack of faith, and Yeshua commented, "Only in his hometown and in his own house is a prophet without honor."

Miracles are only possible when there is a degree of faith on the part of those involved, even if it is the one requesting the miracle, and not the participant, as in the case of the centurion's servant in Matthew 8:5-13.

ODD MAN OUT

Yehudah stood on the river bank and watched Yochanon. The prophet stood knee deep in the water baptizing people who came to him for that purpose. He had been teaching about One who was to come, who would be the one they were waiting for, the Mashiach.

Yehudah had been part of the crowd for several days, listening to Yochanon, who kept saying, even when questioned by the priests, that he was not the one they sought. He was just a voice crying in the wilderness; 'Prepare the Way of HaShem'. One was coming whose sandals he was unworthy to untie.

Yehudah found all this very interesting. Yochanon seemed to him like a great prophet, but if the one who was to follow was to be Ha'Mashiach, then Yehudah could not wait to meet Him. At last perhaps they were going to have someone who would deliver Israel from the hated Roman masters.

Then one day Yochanon looked up and saw his cousin approaching. He was inspired by Ruach Ha'Kodesh to cry out "Behold the Lamb of Elohim!" Yehudah's attention was caught as he saw Yeshua come to Yochanon and ask to be baptized. Yochanon suggested this was happening the wrong way round, but Yeshua insisted. As He came out of the water

Ruach Ha'Kodesh appeared in the form of a dove, and a loud voice said,

"This is My Beloved Son. I am well pleased with Him." Yehudah merely heard what he thought was thunder, but he was impressed enough that he determined that he would follow this man. He decided that for the look of it he had better be baptized as well, though his heart was not really in it.

Yeshua then disappeared into the wilderness for a while, and Yehudah stayed with Yochanon until He returned and collected those whom He was calling to follow Him.

Yochanon watched them go, his disciples going with someone else, but he realized quickly that this was the way it had to be. He was only there to prepare the way for the greater Man.

As the growing crowd followed Yeshua, He started to teach them about what He called the Kingdom of Heaven, and how He was the only Way to that kingdom. To get there you needed to believe in Him, repent and be baptized. Yehudah heard what was being said, but did not take it all in, for his heart was obsessed with the plans he was making for when Yeshua started to lead His army against the Roman oppressors.

Yeshua knew that His Father was telling Him to choose twelve men from those who were following Him to be His close companions. He called those He wanted, including Yehudah among that number. He knew Yehudah's heart, and that one day he would be the man who would betray Him, but that time was a long way off, and He felt that by keeping Yehudah close to Him He would be able to keep an eye on this strange man.

Gradually a group began to surround Yeshua who could contribute to his support and that of his companions. This group included several wealthy women who looked after their needs and supplied their wants. This warranted somebody to look after the common purse, and Yeshua sought one among His group to do this. Yehudah's face lit up. Money! He loved it! He had to get his hands on that money bag. Mattathiyu was suggested, as he had been a tax collector and understood money, but he declined.

"That was my old life, and I am not interested in handling money any more. Let Yehudah do it if he wants to." So Yehudah became the keeper of the money bag. He liked nothing better than to empty the bag and count the contents, and quite often less went back into the bag than was taken out of it, for he was a thief, and would help himself whenever he thought he could get away with it. Yeshua was not deceived though; He knew very well what was going on.

Two or three years passed, with Yeshua and his small band of companions traveling around the Galilee, teaching in the towns and villages they passed through. This green and lush countryside was alien territory to Yehudah, who missed the higher and drier landscape of his home in Kerioth, in Judea. The others in the group listened and learned but Yehudah only listened with half an ear, and learned little. He had other things to do.

They spent most of their time in the Galilee, but visited Yerushalayim two or three times a year for feast days. One day they were in Bethany, and were all invited to dinner at the home of Yeshua's friend Lazarus, whom Yeshua had raised from the dead, and who lived with his two sisters, Miriam and Marta.

As they all reclined at the table with Lazarus, and Marta was serving them, Miriam came up behind Yeshua with a jar of expensive perfume and poured it over his feet, then wiped them with her hair. The sweet fragrance of the perfume filled the house.

Yehudah was not one of those who enjoyed the scent.

He objected, "That perfume was expensive, and you have wasted it! It could have been sold for a year's wages, and the money given to the poor." The truth was that Yehudah cared nothing for the poor, but wanted the money for himself. Yeshua told him to leave Miriam alone.

"This was intended for my burial," He told them. "The poor will always be with you, but I will not be here much longer."

Yehudah grumbled to himself. "This is not going the way it should. Surely by now Yeshua would have started raising the army that would overthrow the Romans. What does He think He is doing?" He needed to think more about what he could do to hurry things along.

It was when Yeshua set out for Yerushalayim for what would be the last time that Yehudah really came to the boil. This was not going right! It was going to be up to him to see that the kingdom he wanted so badly was established. He thought about going to the priests and asking their advice. They did not like the Romans any more than he did.

So it was that one day while they were in the capital Yeshua sent him out with the money bag to buy food for the group. This was his opportunity. He hurried to the house of the high priest, Caiaphas, and asked to speak to him, telling him what was on his mind. Caiaphas and his advisors conferred among themselves and then came to Yehudah with a proposition;

"How do you feel about giving Yeshua into our hands? We would make it worth your while." This offer immediately spoke to Yehudah's covetous heart.

"How much?"

"Twenty pieces of silver." Yehudah thought about this. It was not enough.

"Forty," he countered. "But what would you do with Him when you had Him?"

"Oh," Caiaphas answered casually, "probably just talk to him for a while. Put a little pressure on him by throwing Him in jail for a couple of days to teach Him the error of His ways. And then let Him go with a caution." Yehudah considered this. He really did not want to see Yeshua hurt, because he felt that there was still a great deal of work to be done, and he had grown fond of the Teacher in spite of himself. After a little haggling they agreed on thirty pieces of silver, up front, and Yehudah went on his way with a grim smile on his face.

It was time for the Passover celebration, and Yeshua and his companions planned to eat the Seder meal together. During the meal the conversation came round to the expectation that Yeshua did not have very much longer with them, and that He was going to be betrayed. Kepha signaled to Yochanon, who was seated next to Yeshua, to ask Him who was to be the betrayer. Yeshua indicated that it was Yehudah, and told him to get on and do what he had to do, quickly. Yehudah left the group and hurried out to meet with the priests and tell them this was the time.

After dinner Yeshua and his companions went to a garden called Gethsemane, where there were olive trees. He took Kepha, Ya'aqov and Yochanon and left the others to keep watch. While He was praying to His Father, and agreeing to do what was required of Him, Yehudah approached with a group of temple guards, carrying lanterns and torches and armed with spears. Yeshua faced them without surprise, for He knew they were coming for Him, but confounded them with His confidence. Yehudah betrayed Him with a kiss and then left, his duty done. He did not want to be part of what happened next.

Yeshua was bound and taken to the authorities and ill treated, accused of claiming to be the king of the Jews, which was clearly a trumped up charge amounting to treason. Early next morning He was condemned to death by crucifixion. This was the sentence passed on common criminals who had been found guilty of serious crimes. Yeshua was of course innocent of any wrongdoing. Yehudah received this news with horror; he had never expected such consequences of his actions, and was deeply repentant of what he had done.

He rushed to the priests and screamed at them, "You never said you would crucify Him. You told me you would only put Him in jail for a couple of days. How could you do this!" The priests merely shrugged and ignored him. Yehudah threw the coins they had given him at their feet, rushed out and hanged himself in remorse. The priests gathered up the coins, but because it was blood money they could not return it to the temple, so they used it to buy the field where Yehudah had died as a burial ground for foreigners. When they cut down his body it burst open and his intestines were spilled out. Thus it became known as the Field of Blood, and another prophecy in Scripture was fulfilled.

Judas really was the odd man out. He was the son of Simon Iscariot, which means 'from Kerioth'. Kerioth was a town in Judea, which would make Judas the only one of the Twelve who was not a Galilean. But this was not the only thing which set him apart from the rest of Jesus' closest companions. He had an agenda right from the start. He could never see Jesus as Lord and Master, but only as Rabbi or Teacher. He had little real interest in the Kingdom of Heaven, but was obsessed with the idea of overthrowing the Romans and establishing a kingdom here on earth. Jesus knew from the start who he was and what he would do, but knew too that prophecies in Scripture had to be fulfilled.

HOSANNA

Stefanos was spending time in his father's shop. It was the first day of the week, the morning after Shabbat, not a busy time in the world of commerce, so he stood idly by the open door, thinking of Yeshua, and that maybe it was time he went to see what He was doing these days.

His attention was drawn to what was happening in the street. It was busier than usual, and everyone was hurrying in one direction, towards the Mount of Olives. Something was going on, and he needed to find out what it was.

He made his excuses quickly to his father, and slipped out before anyone could stop him. Baruch just smiled fondly. He and his wife had long indulged their youngest son, letting him get away with disappearing for days at a time. He always came back, full of stories about this man Yeshua, whom they called Rabboni, my Teacher. It was not as though Stefanos needed to work, or to learn to manage the store; his older brother would take over that task one of these days. Sometime Stefanos would grow up and learn responsibility, but that time seemed to be long in coming, and meanwhile Baruch could live with his occasional absences.

Stefanos got caught up in the crowd, and began to question where they were going, and why.

"There is a lot of shouting on the Mount of Olives," he was told, "and we hear some sort of procession is going on." Stefanos started to run with the others, and when they reached the city gate he could hear the shouting and see a great crowd of people heading towards the city. As he neared the scene across the Kidron Valley he could see the throng surrounding someone riding on a donkey, and all kinds of activity surrounding him. He was able to recognize The Teacher as the rider, and the crowd was acclaiming Him as King! They had Him riding on a donkey, had strewn their cloaks in His path, and were waving palm branches and shouting "Hosanna to the son of Dawid! Blessed is the king who comes in the Name of HaShem!

Stefanos fell into step with a man who was singing and dancing with his arms in the air.

"What's going on?" he asked. "Where did all this start?" The man calmed down to tell his story.

"For me it started yesterday," he began. "My friend and I," he indicated another man close by, "were sitting by the side of the road that goes down to Jericho. We were both blind. My friend has been blind from birth, but I used to be able to see. I lost my sight in an accident several years ago. Anyway, we were sitting by the side of the road because we had heard that the Teacher was going to pass on his way to Yerushalayim for the Feast. As the Teacher approached with His companions, we started to shout,

'Yeshua, son of Dawid, have mercy on us'. Some of the people with him wanted to shut us down and not bother Him, but we kept on shouting to attract His attention. Then He called us to come to Him.

So we jumped up and went to Him, and He asked 'What do you want from me?'

'Lord, we want to see', we answered.

At once He said, 'Go, your faith has healed you'. And just like that we were able to see. Eli here is still a bit confused, because he is not yet used to being able to see, but I am just rejoicing that I have my sight back."

He stepped away and started again to dance and wave his arms, praising Yeshua and HaShem. But Stefanos had not finished.

"What's your name?" he asked.

"My father was Timaeus, so they call me Bartimaeus. It used to be Blind Bartimaeus, but they cannot call me that any longer!" He was exultant.

"So then what happened?" Stefanos persevered.

"Well, we decided to follow Him, of course! We all stayed in Bethany last night, and when we got to Bethphage this morning, Yeshua sent two of his companions on ahead to the next village, asking them to bring him a donkey and her colt, which they would find tied there. I went along with them. They saw the animals as He had described, but when they started to untie them, the owners objected, asking what they were doing.

"'The Master has need of them', they were told, and at once the objections ceased and they were allowed to lead the donkey and colt away.

"When they reached The Teacher, someone threw his cloak over the colt and Yeshua sat on it. Then others stripped off their cloaks and spread them in the road ahead of them. Others cut branches from the trees overhead and either spread them as well in the road, or waved them, and everyone started calling out things like, 'Hosanna in the highest', 'Blessed is the coming kingdom of our father Dawid', and 'Blessed is the King of Israel!' They were singing praises for all the miracles they had seen, including mine."

By this time the procession was winding its way down the narrow lane which leads from the Mount of Olives to the Kidron Valley, towards the Temple on the mount which bears its name. Stefanos thought about what he was seeing and hearing. Yeshua the King of the Jews? He didn't think so! This did not agree with what he knew of The Teacher. He could see the humility in the fact that the Teacher was riding on a tiny donkey. Nothing he had heard Yeshua teach about indicated that He had thoughts about leading the Jews into battle against the Roman oppressors. Stefanos remembered all the stories about being meek, and compassionate, and coming as a little child, but while He could be passionate about injustice and sin, it did not sound as though Yeshua was planning to become their earthly king.

The crowd slowly proceeded down the road to the valley, still shouting "Hosanna," and praising the son of Dawid, and when they reached the foot of the Temple Mount, Yeshua had compassion on the donkey and dismounted. He told the disciple who had charge of it, and who had been leading it, to see that the animal was fed and rested, and then returned to the owner, with the Teacher's thanks. Then everyone climbed the hill and entered the Temple. Yeshua looked around Him and grimaced at what He saw, which was table after table of moneylenders, and merchants selling doves and lambs for temple sacrifice. He said nothing and the company returned to Bethany for the night.

Stefanos invited Bartimaeus and his friend home for the night, since they had nowhere else to go, and he wanted to continue their conversation. The three made their way to Stefanos' home, where he presented the two who had been healed of their blindness to his parents, who welcomed them warmly. Over the evening meal they described what had happened that day, and Bartimaeus told his story again. His friend Eli was quieter, still processing his being able to see the world around him, which was very strange to him.

Next morning the three men returned to the Temple area, to await the Teacher and his companions. Yeshua looked grim, and when they all entered the outer courts He grew very angry. He seized a staff from a bystander and started using it to clear all the tables of the merchants and moneylenders, overturning them and sweeping all the money onto the floor. A huge commotion ensued, with escaped doves fluttering around, the sounds of angry shouting mixed with the cries of sacrificial lambs, while the merchants scrambled to sort out the mess, cursing as they scrabbled about on their hands and knees.

"My Father's house is supposed to be a house of prayer!" Yeshua shouted, "But you have made it into a den of thieves."

Stefanos had conflicting emotions; as the son of a merchant he was saddened to see the day's profits spread around for anyone to pick up, but as a follower of Yeshua he had to see the point of what was happening. The outer courts of the temple had become little more than a marketplace, with more commerce taking place than prayer. It was no longer a quiet place of contemplation, but a busy shopping centre.

As Yeshua continued to dismantle the booths of the merchants the temple guards descended on Him, spurred on by the Pharisees, but when they saw that the crowds were protecting Him, they said to one another, "This is getting us nowhere. We will have to wait for another occasion to get Him." Jesus continued to teach the crowds, who were eager to listen to Him.

Stefanos took leave of his new friends, who wanted to return to their own homes; they had so much to tell their families. He walked home slowly, pondering all these happenings, but more sure than ever in his heart that he wanted to be a follower of Yeshua. He was quite determined that he was not going to be a merchant like his father and brother, but would stay with Yeshua as much as he could, and help to care for him.

Jesus taught about the Kingdom of Heaven, but many people listening to him, like Judas, were more concerned with overthrowing their Roman masters and establishing a different kind of kingdom in their land. Stephen was right in his assessment of Jesus and His teachings. Yes, Jesus was King of the Jews, but He was their heavenly King, not an earthly one.

THE HIDDEN DISCIPLE

Yosef was really angry!

His servant had just woken him from a deep sleep to tell him that a special meeting of the Sanhedrin had been called. It was not that fact that enraged him, it was the information that his own relative had been arrested by the temple guard and would be tried for various crimes of which, Yosef knew for a fact, Yeshua was innocent. He would have to see about that, though he knew it would not be easy. His belief in Yeshua was not public knowledge, and it would cost him to defend his nephew.

Yosef grumbled to himself as he dressed and pulled his warm cloak round him before setting off for the house of the high priest, Caiaphas, where the meeting was to be held. It was the middle of the night and he did not appreciate being dragged from his warm bed to attend a meeting which, so far as he was concerned, was a complete waste of time. He had no illusions about Annas and Caiaphas—if these two had made up their minds that Yeshua was guilty of these trumped up charges, there was little anyone else could do about it.

Nikodemus turned a corner and fell into step with Yosef.

"Shalom Aleichem," they greeted one another. "What is all this? You and I know who Yeshua really is, and these charges against him are ridiculous. Don't you remember that time when he was about 12 years old, and He was in the temple talking with the teachers of the law and astounding them with his knowledge and insight?"

The two friends arrived at their destination and took their seats with the rest of the Sanhedrin. Meanwhile Kepha and Yochanon had followed Yeshua and his captors. Most of His companions had fled when He was arrested, but these two followed at a distance. Yochanon was known to the guard, so was allowed into Caiaphas' courtyard, and he persuaded the guards to let Kepha enter as well. They sat down to see what happened. Kepha pretended three times, when challenged, that he was not with Yeshua. He bitterly regretted this statement when the rooster crowed and he was reminded of what Yeshua had said earlier about Kepha denying Him. When all had arrived Yeshua was led in by the temple guards, and Caiaphas read out the charges against him—blasphemy for claiming He was the Mashiach, and inciting the Jews to stop paying taxes to Caesar. Several false witnesses were brought before the Sanhedrin to swear they had heard Yeshua blaspheming and inciting riots.

Yosef was furious; "I have to say something!" he muttered to Nikodemus under his breath. He stood and was given permission to speak. "Gentlemen," he started, "these witnesses are not telling the truth. I have known this man all his life—is not his mother the daughter of my older brother Yoachim? He is totally committed to righteousness. I have heard Him say 'Give unto Caesar the things that are Caesar's'. How is that denying Caesar's right to taxes? As for the blasphemy accusation, He has admitted that He is the Son of Elohim. I think we should let him go." He smiled at his nephew and sat down.

The Sanhedrin was in an uproar.

"He is guilty!" many shouted.

Caiaphas intervened. "As I have said before, it is better for one man to die for many than that all should perish." He ordered the guard to flog Yeshua, bind Him and send Him to Pilate.

Yosef made a point of going to Pilate's house to see what would happen. Pilate asked Yeshua point blank,

"Are you the King of the Jews?"

"Yes, it is as you say," replied Yeshua. The chief priests again made their accusations against Him, but He refused to answer them, to Pilate's amazement.

Pilate's wife approached and asked to speak to her husband privately.

"Have nothing to do with this man," she urged him. "I have had bad dreams about this, and I believe that if you listen to the crowd and hand him over to them, you will be very sorry."

Pilate nodded to her, turned to the crowd and announced, "I can find no fault with him. I understand he is from Galilee. Send him to Herod." Herod was the Tetrarch of Galilee, who was in Jerusalem at the time.

Herod was more curious—he wanted to see Yeshua do miracles, but was not successful in persuading Him to do anything, even answer him, so he mocked and ridiculed Him and sent Him back to Pilate. Pilate suggested that he release Yeshua and convict Barabbas, who was a criminal, instead. But the crowd would have none of this.

"Crucify Him!" they shouted over and over. Pilate wanted to release Him, but the crowd insisted that He be the one who was crucified, and finally Pilate washed his hands publicly and handed Him over to be crucified.

Yosef was following developments closely, hoping there was something he could do, but when he became convinced that no one was prepared to listen to him, he turned away and walked slowly to his house. He had work to do.

After eating something, Yosef dressed himself in his most official clothes; the ones he wore when he went about his business as a Roman metal merchant. He called his servant, gave him instructions and told him to meet him at the crucifixion site.

He returned to the palace where Pilate made his residence. When challenged at the entrance, he said in his most forbidding tones, "Tell Pilate that Nobilis Decurio wishes to see him," using his official title as Minister of Mines to the Roman Government. The guard was impressed and hurried to do his bidding.

When Pilate heard this, he sighed.

"Now what!" but told the guard to send Yosef in. He greeted him formally, and asked, "to what do I owe this pleasure?" Yosef of Arimathea was a wealthy and important man, and a Roman citizen as well, and Pilate could not afford to offend him.

"You have handed a man over to be crucified who is not only innocent, but who is a member of my own family," Yosef announced. "I wish to claim his body for burial."

Pilate was nonplussed. "I don't think so," He answered. "Those who have been crucified are always buried in mass graves, with no markers. They are no longer considered to have any worth." He knew that the authorities wanted Yeshua out of the way, permanently, with no reminders of Who He said He was. In any case, it was unusual for anyone to come forward to claim the body of a criminal who had been executed.

"I must insist," was Yosef's reply. "I am the head of his family, and his closest male relative, and therefore I have the right. Besides," and he drew himself up to his full height, "as a Roman citizen I believe that I can take this matter all the way up to Caesar, if it is necessary." Pilate was deflated; his job was on the line.

The argument continued for a while, but eventually Pilate realized that he would have to give in.

"And," Yosef demanded in confident tones, "I shall need a certificate to show to the captain of the guard at the crucifixion, to prove that I have your permission to take the body of my nephew. And it will have your official seal on it. I have a new tomb in the same area, and I will use that for burial." Pilate nodded nervously and arranged for his scribe to prepare the necessary document immediately.

While this was being done, the two men made small talk. Suddenly there was a loud noise, the ground shook violently, and the room went dark.

"What was that?" Pilate exclaimed, as servants hurried in with lamps.

"Just the work of salvation being completed," was Yosef's reply. Pilate had no idea what Yosef was talking about, but determined to find out what had happened.

When the document was ready, Pilate handed it to Yosef, who took it, thanked him for his courtesy, and left. Pilate breathed a huge sigh of relief. Maybe this would not have repercussions, though he greatly feared he had not heard the last of the matter.

Meanwhile, Yosef collected Nikodemus, saying he would need his friend's help, and telling him to bring his servant with him. They hurried to the crucifixion site, where they found the captain of the Roman guard ensuring that the three crucified men were in fact dead. The next day was to be a special Shabbat, so the bodies could not be left on the crosses after sundown, which was rapidly approaching.

Yosef handed his certificate to the captain of the guard, who nodded his permission for the small group to remove Yeshua's body from the cross and take Him for burial. Yosef, Nikodemus and their servants gently retrieved the body and carried him to the tomb Yosef had mentioned to Pilate, which was not far away. They wrapped Him in the cloths which Yosef's servant had brought, and used some of the burial spices which he had fetched, and laid Yeshua carefully in the tomb. There was no time to do more before all work had to stop for the Shabbat. As they left they rolled a big stone against the entrance to the tomb. It took all four of them to move the stone, which was massive.

"That will have to do for now," murmured Yosef. "He will be safe there until the Shabbat is over, and then we can do the proper embalming." The two friends, followed by their servants, walked sadly and dejectedly home. They had no understanding that by the time they were ready to revisit the tomb Yeshua would have risen from the dead and been seen by several people. This knowledge would bring them great satisfaction in the days to come, as well as great hardship, but for now they had done what they could. Several of Yeshua's close companions had been watching, so they knew where He had been laid, and they were grateful, but it would be a long three days before they would see Him again.

There was great rejoicing three days later when they heard that Yeshua's body had disappeared from the tomb, and it was proved that He had risen from the dead, and was seen and touched by several of his companions. He continued to move among His disciples for forty days, until the day when He was taken up into heaven before their eyes.

There is very little written about Joseph of Arimathea in Scripture, but there are many traditional stories and legends written about this man. It is fairly well established that he was a high councillor and a voting member of the Sanhedrin. He was also a Roman citizen who supplied the Roman

Government with tin and other metals which he arranged to have mined in places like Britain. It is true that only a close relative of Jesus' would have been able to claim His body, as the authorities would have liked to bury Him anonymously, and get rid of Him once and for all. Joseph, as a Roman citizen, and also as His relative, had the power to do so, and Pilate had to give in to him. However, Joseph's act provoked both the Jews and the Romans, and he spent time in prison and was eventually banished for his deeds, according to legend.

153 FISH

Shimon, known also as Kepha, was restless. He had been unhappy for several days, berating himself for the way he had denied knowing Yeshua. Three times, no less. How could he have been so stupid! Yes, Yeshua had risen from the dead, and Kepha and the other disciples had seen him a couple of times, and then the Teacher had said to them, "I am going before you into Galilee."

Therefore the disciples had separated, each going to his own home. Kepha collected his wife and took her to Capernaum, to visit her mother, which was fine for a while, but he could not settle. So one afternoon he said to her, "I am going fishing."

His wife smiled at him; she knew her burly husband well. He had to do something active or go crazy.

Kepha climbed aboard his boat and sailed a few miles east to where the fishing fleet was stationed, in Bethsaida. There he found Ya'aqov and Yochanon, the sons of his father's partner Zebediah, as well as Te'oma, Natan'el and two others of the close group.

"Who wants to go fishing?" he asked. The others agreed that they might as well go with him as sit around waiting for something to happen. Thus they found themselves out on the lake in the middle of the night. When they reached the fishing grounds, or so they thought, they threw their nets into the sea and hauled them in as usual. Nothing. No fish! They tried again and again with the same result. All the fish in the lake seemed to have gone elsewhere! Frustrated in the extreme, they returned to shore.

While they were still some way from land, they saw a man standing on the beach, but did not recognize him. He called out to them,

"Hey there, have you caught any fish?"

"No," they answered, "not a thing."

"Try throwing your net on the right side of the boat," they were told. Kepha shrugged. They had been throwing that net until they were tired, with no results, but he supposed one more time wouldn't hurt. They threw it out as instructed and immediately the net grew heavy. There were so many large fish in it that their combined efforts could not haul it into the boat.

Yochanon was the first to realize Who it was on shore. He said to Kepha, "It is the Master!" Kepha looked at the man more closely and recognized Yeshua. He wrapped himself in his tunic, for he had discarded it while fishing, as it was bulky and got in his way, and jumped into the water to make his way to shore, which was close by. The others followed in the boat, towing the net full of fish. When they got there they found Yeshua standing by a fire of burning coals, where he had been grilling a small fish, with bread waiting nearby.

"Come and have breakfast," He called. "Bring some of the fish you caught." The men were able to drag the net full of fish to shore, which was easier than lifting it into the boat. There were 153 fish in the net, but they were astonished to find that even with so great a load, there were no holes in the net, which was miraculous in itself.

Picking out a few choice fish to grill, they joined Yeshua for breakfast. Kepha approached hesitantly, for he was still not sure of his welcome after what he felt was his betrayal of the Teacher. Yeshua however knew what Kepha was thinking, and resolved to reinstate him as soon as possible. After a companionable meal of bread and fish, while Kepha was standing close to the fire in an attempt to dry his wet clothes, Yeshua turned to him and asked, "Shimon ben Yonatan, do you really love me more than these?"

"Yes, Master," Kepha answered, "you know I love you."

"Feed my lambs," Yeshua replied.

Kepha was silent. *Feed my lambs, He said.* What did He mean? This would require thought, something that did not come naturally to the fisherman except insofar as his work was concerned.

Again Yeshua asked, "Shimon ben Yonatan, do you really love me?" Kepha was surprised to be asked this a second time.

"Yes, Master, you know that I love you."

"Take care of my sheep." And a third time the question came, "Shimon ben Yonatan, do you love me?"

This really hurt Kepha, to be asked a third time, but he answered, "Master, you know all things. You know that I love you."

"Feed my sheep," he was told.

Suddenly Kepha realized what was happening; he had denied three times that he knew the Teacher, so he had to affirm three times that he loved Him. He was back in Yeshua's good graces. His dark mood left him, and he started to dance.

Yeshua smiled fondly; His black sheep had returned to Him. He continued, "Listen now to what I am telling you. When you are young you are able to look after yourself and go where you wish, but when you are old others will stretch out your hands and take you where you do not want to go." He was letting Kepha know that he too would die by crucifixion, but that because He Himself had gone this way before, Kepha would be able to handle it with grace. "Follow me," He concluded.

Up until now, Peter had simply been one of Jesus' companions, albeit one of the three closest to the Teacher, along with James and John. But after this time of reinstatement he became the acknowledged leader of the band. He was a simple fisherman to start with, though he had some education in the Torah, as all Jewish children did, but on the Day of Pentecost he became a leader and eloquent teacher in his own right. He traveled widely proclaiming the Kingdom of God, was the first to realize that this Good News was for the Gentiles as well as the Jews, and was eventually martyred for the cause. Tradition says that because he felt unworthy of a death like that of Jesus, he insisted on being crucified upside down.

EPILOGUE

SHAVUOT

Stefanos arose early in order to sneak out of the house. He really did not need to bump into his father this morning.

Baruch was starting to mutter, "Enough already of this foolishness! The man Yeshua is gone—crucified, resurrected, ascended into heaven—whatever. But He is history, and perhaps it is time you settled down and did a job of work for a change."

Stefanos knew that his father loved him, and gave him a great deal of freedom, but he was not ready yet to settle down and work in the shop. Yeshua may no longer be with them, but He had left a rich legacy of teaching, and Stefanos planned to spend as much time as possible in the company of those who had known Him best.

He hurried down the street towards his destination. All the followers of Yeshua had agreed to meet this morning in an Upper Room. It was the first day of the week, just ten days since the Teacher had disappeared for the last time, and his followers met every day to talk about what was next for them.

Stefanos was one of the first to arrive, but Kepha and several of the remaining Eleven companions were talking quietly in a corner. Gradually others made their way into the great vaulted room; his cousin Natan'el, one of the Eleven, several of the women, including Salome and Miriam from Magdala. Yochanon entered, supporting Miriam, Yeshua's mother, and then Lazarus arrived with his sisters; another Miriam and Marta.

One familiar figure was missing. Yosef of Arimathea was in prison. His actions on the day of Yeshua's death had so annoyed both the Roman and Jewish authorities that he had been sent to prison, though he was due to be released soon. As a Roman citizen he had certain rights, and it would do nobody any good to punish him beyond a certain point.

About a hundred and twenty people had assembled in the upper room when Kepha, who seemed to have assumed leadership of the group, closed the doors and called for order. He started talking about Yeshua, the Teacher, and how He had said "Stay in Yerushalayim until you receive the gift my Father has promised…in a few days you will be baptized with the Ruach Ha'Kodesh."

"There is little we can do at present," Kepha informed them, "but Yeshua did promise that He would send us help. He talked about the Comforter, and we all know we need comfort after the events of the last few weeks, but I feel that there is something more that will happen if we are just patient, though we do not know yet what that will look like."

At that moment a sound was heard, like a wind blowing in the distance. Everyone stopped and listened to it. It appeared to come closer, gathering in strength, until suddenly it roared through the room, affecting all who were there, and throwing loose objects into the air where they whirled around before settling. There was a corporate gasp as everyone inhaled, and then the wind disappeared as abruptly as it had arrived, leaving tongues of fire which appeared to dance around the room, touching and resting on everyone's head. A great excitement broke out, and everybody started talking at once. It was immediately evident that they were not speaking their native language, but a variety of alien tongues.

Stefanos felt light-headed, and could not stop himself talking. He could not understand what he was saying, but soon realized that HaShem understood him, and that his spirit was communicating directly with HaShem's Ruach.

In their excitement they threw open the heavy doors and spilled out into the area outside, which happened to be part of a busy marketplace. There were hundreds of men and women there, from all parts of the known world, buying and selling their goods and wares. People from Persia, Mesopotamia, Rome, Egypt and Libya, Asia and Arabia were utterly amazed as they heard these excited Jews speaking in their own languages and declaring the wonders of HaShem.

"What does this mean?" they asked one another in bewilderment. Several however laughed and mocked the disciples, saying to one another, "These people have really been drinking too much wine!"

Kepha heard this and approached the mockers. He and the Eleven stood together and he declared, "Now fellow Jews, and the rest of you who are visiting, listen carefully to what I am about to tell you. These men are not drunk as you suppose; it is after all only nine in the morning. No, you are seeing the fulfillment of a prophecy by the prophet Yoel, who said that HaShem promised that in the last days He would '…pour out My Ruach on all people. Your sons and daughters will prophesy, your young men will see visions, your old men will dream dreams…and everyone who calls on the Name of Elohim will be saved.'"

Kepha went on to speak eloquently about Yeshua and how the Jews had killed Him by nailing Him to the cross, but that after three days He had risen again, because death found it impossible to keep its hold on Him. He reminded them of Dawid, a patriarch whose story was known to all Jews, and how when he died, he was buried and his tomb was known, but HaShem had promised him that He would put his descendants on the throne. Now Yeshua was no longer in his tomb, but had risen from the dead and ascended to His Father in heaven, and just a few minutes ago, had sent the promised Ruach Ha'Kodesh to continue to teach that Yeshua was both Elohim and Ha'Mashiach.

Stefanos privately whispered to his cousin Natan'el, "Kepha was just a rough fisherman when he first started following Yeshua, but listen to him now! He has suddenly become a teacher in his own right." Natan'el nodded, but was too overwhelmed by the morning's events to answer coherently.

The crowd heard Kepha insisting that they all needed to repent and be baptized for the forgiveness of their sins, at which time they would receive the gift of the Ruach Ha'Kodesh; all whom Elohim would call. A large number clamored for Kepha to baptize them, declaring that they believed in Yeshua Ha'Mashiach, and were sorry for what they had done, about three thousand of them becoming new believers. Truly a new Church was born that day.

As the days passed, the disciples spent most of their time together, teaching, praying and eating with each other. Several people sold some of their possessions so that they could all live communally. Stefanos left his father's house after a big argument, and joined the rest of the disciples, contributing what he could to their mutual support. Many miracles were seen to be done, and all lived simply, continuing faithfully under the teaching of the apostles. The people of Yerushalayim looked on them with favor, and many came to believe in Yeshua, were saved, and joined the fledgling church.

One day several of the believers, led by Kepha and Yochanon, went up to the temple to pray together. Stefanos was with them. At the Gate Beautiful they came upon a man, lame from birth, who sat at the gate daily begging for alms. Kepha said to him, "Look at us." When he gave them his attention, expecting to receive some charity, Kepha continued, "I don't have any money for you, but I can give you what I do have. In the name of Yeshua Ha'Mashiach of Natzarat, get up and walk!" He took the beggar by the hand and helped him stand, and at once the man's feet and ankles gained strength, and he was able to walk. In fact he ran and danced his way into the temple, praising HaShem. The people who saw this were amazed, since they recognized him as the beggar who sat by the Gate Beautiful every day. Kepha took the opportunity once more to talk about Yeshua, and how it was He who had healed the beggar, not Kepha himself, and again many came to believe in Yeshua.

HELEN THORNTON

KEPHA HELPS A LAME MAN

All this greatly displeased the priests and Jewish authorities, who did their best to stop the disciples, and arrested several of them, holding them in prison overnight. Kepha made an impassioned plea, and the authorities let them go, but forbade them to teach in the Name of Yeshua. This of course had little effect on the apostles, who declared boldly that they couldn't help but teach this way, and because by this time most of the crowds were glorifying HaShem the authorities had little choice but to threaten them and then let them go.

Stefanos was of course in the middle of all this, learning and gaining wisdom, and showing himself to be full of the Ruach Ha'Kodesh.

After a while, the apostles and the rest of the disciples found themselves distributing food daily to the widows and orphans, until one day some of the Greeks complained that their widows were being ignored in favor of the Jews.

Kepha threw up his hands, exclaiming, "Now they are expecting us to do everything. Our role is not to wait at tables, but to spend time in prayer and the Word of HaShem." So the apostles summoned the believers and suggested that they appoint seven whom they would call deacons, men of good reputation, who were filled with the Ruach, to look after the daily distribution of food., This meant that the Twelve—for Matthias had been appointed to fill the vacancy left by the departure of Yehudah—were able to devote themselves to prayer and ministering the Word. Stefanos and six others were chosen for this work.

Stefanos thoroughly enjoyed his new job. He spent his time organizing what turned out to be a food bank, and became popular with the widows and orphans who attended daily. He especially liked working with the children, seeing those who were thin and malnourished grow strong under the care of the deacons, telling them stories of Yeshua Ha'Mashiach, and watching them come to faith in Him. He was able, under the influence of the Ruach Ha'Kodesh, to do many miracles, and saw signs and wonders taking place around him.

He returned to his father's house and became reconciled to his father, whom he loved. Both had suffered under the estrangement, but Baruch relented when he realized that Stefanos was in fact doing an honest job of work, and was not simply wasting his time. It just was not the kind of work that he envisaged his son doing, but Stefanos was happy and that was the most important thing.

Later on Stephen became the first Christian martyr. Some who disputed with him paid false witnesses to swear that they had heard him saying blasphemous things about Moses and God. They incited the people, the elders and scribes, who seized him and brought him before the council. He spoke eloquently before the Sanhedrin, but what he said further inflamed the crowd, and eventually they took him out and stoned him to death.

GO INTO ALL THE WORLD…

Philippos found himself walking along a dusty road in the heat of the day, and wondered what on earth he was doing there. After Stephanos' death Sha'ul persecuted the disciples without mercy and most of them had scattered to different parts of the country.

Philippos went to Samaria and started preaching the Gospel there, with great success, but an angel had appeared to him and told him to go down to the desert road that led from Yerushalayim to Gaza, and he had departed immediately.

Now here he was on that desert road, trudging south, with the sun in his eyes. He was tired and thirsty, after several days on the road from Samaria, and had no idea why he was supposed to be there.

Far in the distance he could see a grove of palm trees. That meant there would be shade, some water, and he hoped he would find some dates on the trees. He looked forward to reaching the oasis, but however long he walked, it never seemed to get any nearer. Automatically he greeted fellow travelers with

"Shalom," and received a greeting in reply,

"Shalom aleichem," but there was no stopping to talk; it was too hot.

After a while, Philippos heard a new sound behind him. It was the sound of hoofbeats and wheels turning, and above this, a high voice declaiming some of the words of the prophet Isaiah. He turned to look and saw an imposing chariot drawn by two magnificent horses. Seated behind the driver was an Ethiopian, obviously a man of some importance. That was nothing particularly unusual, but what was different was that this man held a scroll and was reading aloud as he traveled.

Philippos stood still and watched as the carriage approached. The Ruach Ha'Kodesh told him to stay nearby and see what happened.

Seeing Philippos' interest, and recognizing him as a Jew, and probably an educated one, the Ethiopian acknowledged him with a word of greeting.

"Do you understand what you are reading?" Philippos asked.

"No, and I don't have anyone to explain it to me," was the reply.

"Perhaps I can help."

"Please join me in this carriage and we can travel together and talk as we go."

The Ethiopian gave orders for the carriage to stop, and Philippos climbed in and sat down opposite his host.

"You were reading from the scroll of the prophet Isaiah," he started.

"Yes. I am a believer in the one true Elohim, and I went to Yerushalayim to worship Him, because that is where we are told we need to go to worship Him. While there I was able to purchase this scroll, so that I might learn more, and I have been reading this prophet Isaiah. He says, 'He was led like a sheep to the slaughter, and as a lamb before the shearer is silent, so he did not open his mouth.' What does that mean? Was he talking about himself or someone else?"

Philippos started to explain, "As a prophet, Isaiah was pointing towards a happening in the future. He was talking about One who would come to redeem mankind, and to save us from our sins.

"About four years ago a new Teacher appeared. His Name was Yeshua, but we called him Rabboni, which means My Teacher. He collected a small band of men around Him, and I was privileged to be one of them, so I knew Him well, and traveled around with Him, listening to Him teach. He also did many signs and wonders, miracles of healing for many people, and even raised several from the dead!"

The Ethiopian was fascinated by what he heard.

"Tell me more about this man, this Rabboni."

"He told us that He was the Son of the Father, HaShem, Who sent him to earth especially to show us the way to eternal life. He said that He Himself was The Way, and that we should believe in Him. The more we heard Him teach, the more we came to believe that He was in fact the Son of Elohim, come to earth in human form, and that His mandate was to defeat the powers of evil, and bring us all to salvation so that we might live forever with Him in Heaven.

"One of the things He told us is that 'Elohim so loved the world, and the people in it, that He sent His only Son, Yeshua Himself, to be sacrificed on our behalf, so that death might be defeated, once and for all, and that whoever believed in Him might not perish, but have eternal life'."

"So what happened to this Yeshua, this Rabboni? Where is He now?"

"It all happened just as Isaiah prophesied so many years ago. Because so many people started to believe in Him, the authorities became anxious. They were afraid that He might rally the people against our Roman oppressors, and cause them to come down on us with great suffering. So they arrested Him and tried Him for treason. Of course He was quite innocent of that, but He was tried anyway, found guilty, and then crucified."

"No!" The Ethiopian was aghast at this news. So then what happened?"

"He was supposed to be buried in a mass grave and then forgotten. But one of his relatives, a rich man and a Roman citizen, managed to get permission to take down His body, and buried Him in his own tomb, with a big stone at the entrance to prevent anyone stealing Him.

"Then three days later, after the Shabbat, several of the women went to the tomb to anoint Him with spices, only to find the stone rolled away, with an angel sitting on it. He told them not to bother looking for the body, because Yeshua had risen from the dead, and they would see Him sooner or later.

"That very day several people saw Him, and spoke with Him, and some even touched Him. We saw Him eat, and He spent time with us, still teaching. Then after forty days, we saw Him taken up into heaven, where we believe He is now sitting at the right hand of HaShem in all His glory."

"That is some story," said his enthralled listener.

As he spoke, the chariot drew alongside the oasis that Philippos had seen earlier in the distance. The tired horses slowed down, as they could see and smell the water, and hoped for a drink and a rest. The Ethiopian was a compassionate man, and ordered his driver to pull into the shade and stop for a while.

"Let us alight and sit in the shade and continue our discussion," he said.

This they did, and while the horses drank their fill and then grazed on the grass, the servant unpacked a basket of food and set some before the two men, taking his share and withdrawing a short distance to give them privacy.

"So is that the end of the story?" asked the official.

"Not at all," was the answer. "Ten days after Yeshua was taken up into heaven, about a hundred and twenty of us believers were gathered in a room in Yerushalayim, praising HaShem and praying, when the Ruach that Yeshua had told us to expect fell on us, like a great wind. It blew through the room, and it seemed that tongues of fire appeared on everyone's head. We all started speaking in languages that were not our own. It was really strange! Since then we have all been able to talk with boldness about the kingdom of Elohim, and about Yeshua and what He was teaching, and many thousands of people have started to believe and been baptized. You must have run into some of them while you were in the city."

"I suppose I did, but I was mostly in the Temple, and there was not much evidence of that Ruach that you mention there."

"No, we were teaching mainly in the marketplace. The Temple authorities are still very wary of us, and do not understand what is going on. In fact there is a group now which is persecuting us, and trying to kill us or throw us in prison, so many of us have scattered and now teach in other parts of the country. I myself was in Samaria until a few days ago when HaShem told me to take this road south, where I met you."

The Ethiopian was silent for a moment, thinking. Then he spoke again.

"What you have said is very compelling, and touches me deeply. Look, right here is a pool of water. Why shouldn't I be baptized?"

"Philippos replied, "If you believe with all your heart, you may."

"I believe that Yeshua Ha'Mashiach is the Son of Elohim."

Then both men went down into the water and Philippos baptized his companion. As they came up out of the water,

HaShem took Philippos away, and the Ethiopian did not see him again. He turned to thank him, but he was nowhere to be seen.

"Did you see what happened?" he asked his servant.

"No, Master," the servant replied. "He was there, and then he was not."

"But you heard all that he was saying. You have been here all the time."

"Oh, yes, and I think that I believe now as well, although I had no faith before that HaShem even existed."

The Ethiopian official and his servant both gave thanks to HaShem, and went on their way rejoicing. They knew that they had been given a mandate to take the Good News about Yeshua and His Kingdom down to their home in Ethiopia, and vowed to do all they could to spread the news wherever they found themselves.

In Matthew 28 we are told to 'go and make disciples of all nations'. This story is the first one about carrying the Gospel beyond the borders of Galilee and Judea. The Coptic Christians of the Nile Valley, including Egypt and Ethiopia, have a long history. Many of them belong to the Coptic Orthodox Church, or the Coptic Catholic Church, and there is a large colony of the former living in Jerusalem at this time.

GLOSSARY OF NAMES

Listed here are many names and Hebrew words which might not be familiar to the reader.

Following each name is its pronunciation, modern equivalent and meaning.

Elohim: ElOim, **GOD**
El Shaddai: El ShaddEYE, **GOD ALMIGHTY**
HaShem: HaShEm, **GOD**
Rabboni: RabbOneye, Teacher (Jesus), My Teacher
Ruach Ha'Kodesh: Ruakh Ha'KodEsh, The Holy Spirit

PEOPLE
Aharon: AhAHron, Aaron, Priest
Andri: Andri, Andrew, Man
Ari: Ari, Ariel, Lion
Baruch: BarOOk, Baruch, Blessed
Binyamin: BInyamin, Benjamin, Son of the south
Dan'yyel: DahneeEL, Daniel, God is my judge
Dawid: DavEEd, David, Beloved
Eleazar: EleAYzar, Lazarus, My God has helped
Eli: EElie, Eli, Ascension
Elisheva: ElIsheva, Elizabeth, My God is an oath
Esther: Esther, Esther, Star (Persian)
Ezra: Ezra, Ezra, Help
Gidon: GIdon, Gideon, Feller or hewer
Kalev: KAYlev, Caleb, Dog
Kepha: KEpha, Peter, Rock
Leah: LAYah, Leah, Weary
Lydia: LIdia, Lydia, (Greek), Woman from Lydia
Marta: MAHta, Martha, Lady (Aramaic)
Matthias: MatthIas, Matthias, Gift of Yahweh

Mattithayu: MattithAHyu, Matthew, Gift of Yahweh
Miriam or Myriam: Miriam, Mary, Sea of bitterness OR Wished for child
Moshe: MOshe, Moses, Son OR Deliver
Nahum: NAYum, Nahum, Comfort
Natan: NAtan, Nathan, Giver
Natan'el: NatAn'el, Nathaniel, God has given
Nikodemus: NikodEEmus, Nicodemus, Victory of the people (Greek)
Philippos: PhIlippos, Philip, Friend of horses
Rachel: RahKEL, Rachel, Ewe
Rivqah: RIvka, Rebekah OR Rebecca, Snare
Reuven: ROOven, Reuben, Behold, a Son
Salome: SAlomay, Salome, Peace
Sarah: SAHrah, Sarah, Lady OR Princess
Sha'ul: ShAHul, Saul, Prayed For
Shemu'el: ShemU'el, Samuel, Name of God OR God has heard
Shimon: ShimOn, Simon OR Simeon, Hearkening
Shoshanna: ShoshAnnah: Susannah, Lily OR Rose
Stephanos: StephAHnos, Stephen, Crown (Greek)
Te'oma: Te'Oma, Thomas, Twin
Thaddeus: ThaddEEus, Edward, Heard (Aramaic)
Ya'aqov: YAHkov, James or Jacob, Supplanter
Yeshua: YeshUa, Jesus, Yahweh is Salvation
Yoel: YoEl, Joel, Yahweh is God
Yehudah: YehUdah, Judah or Judas, Praised
Yitz'haq: YItzhaq, Isaac, He laughs
Yochanon: YohAnon, John, Yahweh is gracious
Yosef: YOsef, Joseph, He will enlarge
Yonatan: YOnatan, Jonah or Jonathan, Yahweh has given
Zebadiah: ZebedIah, Zebedee, (Unknown)
Zecharya: ZecharIah, Zechariah, Yahweh remembers

PLACES
Beit Lechem is Bethlehem
Mitzrayim is Egypt

THEY CALLED HIM RABBONI

Natzarat is Nazareth
Yerushalayim is Jerusalem

OTHER WORDS
Abba: Abba, Father, Daddy
Chanukah: HAHnukah, Chanukah, Feast of Lights
Ima: EEma, Mother
Mitzvah: Mitzvah, Covenant
Barmitzvah: Coming of age for a boy
(Batmitzvah: Coming of age for a girl)
Mashiach: MashEEakh, Messiah, Christ
Matzah, (pl) matzot:**MAH**tzah, Unleavened bread
Mitzrim: MItzrim, Egyptian(s)
Pesach: PEsahkh, Passover
Seder: Seder, Special Passover meal
Shabbat: ShabbAT, Sabbath, 7th day of the week
Shalom: ShalOHM, Peace, a greeting
Shavuot: ShavuOHT, Pentecost
Sukkot: SukkOHT, Feast of Booths, or Tabernacles